# THE STEAM MAN
## OF THE PRAIRIES

Edward S. Ellis

DOVER PUBLICATIONS, INC.
Mineola, New York

*Bibliographical Note*

This Dover edition, first published in 2016, is an unabridged, newly reset republication of the work originally published in the August 1868 edition of Beadle's American Novel, No. 45. Grammar and style vagaries derive from the source, and are retained here for the sake of authenticity.

*International Standard Book Number*

*ISBN-13: 978-0-486-80613-6*
*ISBN-10: 0-486-80613-8*

Manufactured in the United States by RR Donnelley
80613801  2016
www.doverpublications.com

# Contents

# CHAPTER I

## The Terror of the Prairies

"Howly vargin! what is that?" exclaimed Mickey McSquizzle, with something like horrified amazement.

"By the Jumping Jehosiphat, naow if that don't, beat all natur'!"

"It's the divil, broke loose, wid full steam on!"

There was good cause for these exclamations upon the part of the Yankee and Irishman, as they stood on the margin of Wolf Ravine, and gazed off over the prairie. Several miles to the north, something like a gigantic man could be seen approaching, apparently at a rapid gait for a few seconds, when it slackened its speed, until it scarcely moved.

Occasionally it changed its course, so that it went nearly at right angles. At such times, its colossal proportions were brought out in full relief, looking like some Titan as it took its giant strides over the prairie.

The distance was too great to scrutinize the phenomenon closely; but they could see that a black volume of smoke issued either from its mouth or the top of its head, while it was drawing behind it a sort of carriage, in which a single man was seated, who appeared to control the movements of the extraordinary being in front of him.

No wonder that something like superstitious have filled the breasts of the two men who had ceased hunting for gold, for a few minutes, to view the singular apparition; for such a thing had scarcely been dreamed of at that day, by the most imaginative philosophers; much less had it ever entered the head of these two men on the western prairies.

1

"Begorrah, but it's the ould divil, hitched to his throttin 'waging, wid his ould wife howlding the reins!" exclaimed Mickey, who had scarcely removed his eyes from the singular object.

"That there critter in the wagon is a man," said Hopkins, looking as intently in the same direction. "It seems to me," he added, a moment later, "that there's somebody else a-sit-ting alongside of him, either a dog or a boy. Wal, naow, ain't that queer?"

"Begorrah! begorrah! do ye hear that? What shall we do?"

At that instant, a shriek like that of some agonized giant came home to them across the plains, and both looked around, as if about to flee in terror; but the curiosity of the Yankee restrained him. His practical eye saw that whatever it might be, it was a human contrivance, and there could be nothing supernatural about it.

"Look!"

Just after giving its ear-splitting screech, it turned straight toward the two men, and with the black smoke rapidly puffing from the top of its head, came tearing along at a tremendous rate.

Mickey manifested some nervousness, but he was restrained by the coolness of Ethan, who kept his position with his eye fixed keenly upon it.

Coming at such a railroad speed, it was not long in passing the intervening space. It was yet several hundred yards distant, when Ethan Hopkins gave Mickey a ringing slap upon the shoulder.

"Jerusalem! who do ye s'pose naow, that man is sitting in the carriage and holding the reins?"

"Worrah, worrah! why do you ax me, whin I'm so frightened entirely that I don't know who I am myself?"

"It's Baldy."

"Git out!" replied the Irishman, but added the next moment, "am I shlaping or dhraming? It's Baldy or his ghost."

It certainly was no ghost, judging from the manner in which it acted; for he sat with his hat cocked on one side, a pipe in his mouth, and the two reins in his hands, just as the skillful driver controls the mettlesome horses and keeps them well in hand.

He was seated upon a large pile of wood, while near nestled a little hump-backed, bright-eyed boy, whose eyes sparkled with delight at the performance of the strange machine.

The speed of the steam man gradually slackened, until it came opposite the men, when it came to a dead halt, and the grinning

"Baldy," as he was called, (from his having lost his scalp several years before, by the Indians), tipped his hat and said:

"Glad to see you hain't gone under yit. How'd you git along while I was gone?"

But the men were hardly able to answer any questions yet, until they had learned something more about the strange creation before them. Mickey shied away, as the timid steed does at first sight of the locomotive, observing which, the boy (at a suggestion from Baldy), gave a string in his hand a twitch, whereupon the nose of the wonderful thing threw out a jet of steam with the sharp screech of the locomotive whistle. Mickey sprung a half dozen feet backward, and would have run off at full speed down the ravine, had not Ethan Hopkins caught his arm.

"What's the matter, Mickey, naow! Hain't you ever heard anything like a locomotive whistle?"

"Worrah, worrah, now, but is that the way the crather blows its nose? It must have a beautiful voice when it shnores at night."

Perhaps at this point a description of the singular mechanism should be given. It was about ten feet in hight, measuring to the top of the "stove-pipe hat," which was fashioned after the common order of felt coverings, with a broad brim, all painted a shiny black. The face was made of iron, painted a black color, with a pair of fearful eyes, and a tremendous grinning mouth. A whistle-like contrivance was made to answer for the nose. The steam chest proper and boiler, were where the chest in a human being is generally supposed to be, extending also into a large knapsack arrangement over the shoulders and back. A pair of arms, like projections, held the shafts, and the broad flat feet were covered with sharp spikes, as though he were the monarch of baseball players. The legs were quite long, and the step was natural, except when running, at which time, the bolt uprightness in the figure showed different from a human being.

In the knapsack were the valves, by which the steam or water was examined. In front was a painted imitation of a vest, in which a door opened to receive the fuel, which, together with the water, was carried in the wagon, a pipe running along the shaft and connecting with the boiler.

The lines which the driver held controlled the course of the steam man; thus, by pulling the strap on the right, a deflection was caused which turned it in that direction, and the same acted on the other side. A small rod, which ran along the right shaft, let out or shut off the steam, as was desired, while a cord, running along the left, controlled the whistle at the nose.

The legs of this extraordinary mechanism were fully a yard apart, so as to avoid the danger of its upsetting, and at the same time, there was given more room for the play of the delicate machinery within. Long, sharp, spike-like projections adorned those toes of the immense feet, so that there was little danger of its slipping, while the length of the legs showed that, under favorable circumstances, the steam man must be capable of very great speed.

After Ethan Hopkins had somewhat familiarized himself with the external appearance of this piece of mechanism, he ventured upon a more critical examination.

The door being opened in front, showed a mass of glowing coals lying in the capacious abdomen of the giant; the hissing valves in the knapsack made themselves apparent, and the top of the hat or smoke-stack had a sieve-like arrangement, such as is frequently seen on the locomotive.

There were other little conveniences in the way of creating a draft, and of shutting it off when too great, which could scarcely be understood without a scrutiny of the figure itself.

The steam man was a frightful looking object, being painted of a glossy black, with a pair of white stripes down its legs, and with a face which was intended to be of a flesh color, but, which was really a fearful red.

To give the machinery an abundance of room, the steam man was exceedingly corpulent, swelling out to aldermanic proportions, which, after all, was little out of harmony with its immense hight.

The wagon dragged behind was an ordinary four-wheeled vehicle, with springs, and very strong wheels, a framework being arranged, so that when necessary it could be securely covered. To guard against the danger of upsetting it was very broad, with low wheels, which it may be safely said were made to "hum" when the gentleman got fairly under way.

Such is a brief and imperfect description of this wonderful steam man, as it appeared on its first visit to the Western prairies.

# CHAPTER II

## "Handle Me Gently"

When Ethan Hopkins had surveyed the steam man fully, he drew a long sigh and exclaimed:

"Wal, naow, that's too bad!"

"What's that?" inquired Bicknell, who had been not a little amused at his open-mouthed amazement.

"Do you know I've been thinking of that thing for ten years, ever since I went through Colt's pistol factory in Hartford, when I was a youngster?"

"Did you ever think of any plan!"

"I never got it quite right, but I intended to do it after we got through digging for gold. The thing was just taking shape in my head. See here, naow, ain't you going to give a fellow a ride?"

"Jis' what I wanted; shall I run it for you?"

"No, I see how it works; them 'ere thingumbobs and gimcracks do it all."

"Johnny, hyar, will tell yer 'bout it."

The little humpback sprung nimbly down, and ran around the man, explaining as well as he could in a few moments the manner of controlling its movements. The Yankee felt some sensitiveness in being instructed by such a tiny specimen, and springing into the wagon, exclaimed:

"Git eout! tryin' to teach yer uncle! I knowed how the thing would work before you were born!"

Perching himself on the top of the wood which was heaped up in the wagon, the enthusiastic New Englander carefully looked over the prairie to see that the way was clear, and was about to "let on steam," when he turned toward the Irishman.

"Come, Mickey, git up here."

"Arrah now, but I never learnt to ride the divil when I was home in the ould country," replied the Irishman, backing away.

But both Ethan and Baldy united in their persuasions, and finally Mickey consented, although with great trepidation. He timidly climbed upon the wagon and took his seat beside the Yankee, looking very much as a man may be supposed to look who mounts the hearse to attend his own funeral.

"When yer wants to start, jist pull that 'ere gimcrack!" said Baldy, pointing to the crook in the rod upon which his hand rested.

"Git eout, naow! do you think you're goin' to teach me that has teached school fur five year in Connecticut?"

There were some peculiarities about the steam man which made him a rather unwieldy contrivance. He had a way of starting with a jerk, unless great skill was used in letting on steam; and his stoppage was equally sudden, from the same cause.

When the Irishman and Yankee had fairly ensconced themselves on their perch, the latter looked carefully round to make sure that no one was in the way, and then he turned the valve, which let on a full head of steam.

For a second the monster did not stir. The steam had not fairly taken "hold" yet; then he raised one immense spiked foot and held it suspended in air.

"That's a great contrivance, ain't it?" exclaimed Ethan, contemptuously.

"Can't do nothin' more than lift his foot. Wait till you see more! he's goin' to dance and skip like a lamb, or outrun any locomotive you ever sot eyes on!"

"Bad luck to the loikes of yees, why d' yees go on?" exclaimed the irate Irishman, as he leaned forward and addressed the obdurate machine. "Are yees tryin' to fool us, bad luck to yees?"

At this instant, the feet of the steam man began rising and falling with lightning like rapidity, the wagon being jerked forward with such sudden swiftness, that both Ethan and Mickey turned back summersets, rolling heels over head off the vehicle to the ground, while the monster went puffing over the prairie, and at a terrific rate. Baldy was about to start in pursuit of it, when Johnny, the deformed boy, restrained him.

"It won't run far; the steam is nearly out."

"Be jibbers! but me head is caved in!" exclaimed the Irishman, rising to his feet, rubbing his head, and looking at his hand to see whether there was blood upon it.

"Jerusalem! I thought she had upset or busted her b'iler!" said the Yankee, looking around him with a bewildered air.

The two spectators were laughing furiously, and they could scarcely stand the trick which had been played upon them.

"Let your old machine go to blazes!" muttered Ethan. "If it acts that way, I don't want nothin' to do with it."

In the mean time the steamer had gone rattling over the prairie, until about a quarter of a mile distant, when it rapidly slackened, and as quickly halted.

"What's the matter wid it now?" asked Mickey; "has it got the cramps and gi'n out?"

"The steam is used up!" replied the dwarf, as he hurried after it; "we can soon start it again!"

All four made all haste toward the stationary figure; but the light frame and superior activity of little Johnny brought him to it considerably in advance of the others. Emptying a lot of wood from the wagon, he was busily engaged in throwing it into his stomach when the other two came up. His eyes sparkled, as he said:

"Jump up there, and I'll give you all a ride!"

The three clambered up and took their seats with great care, Mickey and Ethan especially clinging as if their life depended on it.

Johnny threw in the fuel until the black smoke poured in a stream from the hat. Before leaving it, he opened two smaller doors, at the knees, which allowed the superfluous cinders and ashes to fall out. The water in the boiler was then examined, and found all right. Johnny mounted in his place, and took charge.

"Now we are ready! hold fast!"

"Begorrah, if I goes I takes the wagon wid me," replied Mickey, as he closed his teeth and hung on like death.

The engineer managed the monster with rare skill, letting on a full head of steam, and just as it made a move shutting it off, and letting it on almost immediately, and then shutting off and admitting it again, until it began moving at a moderate pace, which, however, rapidly increased until it was going fully thirty miles an hour.

Nothing could be more pleasant than this ride of a mile over the prairie. The plain was quite level, and despite the extraordinary speed attained, the wagon glided almost as smoothly as if running upon a railroad. Although the air was still, the velocity created a stiff breeze about the ears of the four seated on the top of the wood.

The hight of the steam man's head carried the smoke and cinders clear of those behind, while the wonderful machinery within, worked with a marvelous exactness, such as was a source of continued amazement to all except the little fellow who had himself constructed the extraordinary mechanism. The click of the joints as they obeyed their motive power was scarcely audible, and, when once started, there was no unevenness at all in its progress.

When the party had ridden about a half-mile, Johnny described a large circle, and finally came back to the starting, checking the progress with the same skill that he had started it. He immediately sprung down, examined the fire, and several points of the man, when finding everything right, he opened his knee-caps and let cinders and ashes drop out.

"How kin yeou dew that?" inquired Ethan Hopkins, peering over his shoulder.

"What's to hinder?"

"How kin he work his legs, if they're holler that way and let the fire down 'em?"

"They ain't hollow. Don't you see they are very large, and there is plenty of room for the leg-rods, besides leaving a place for the draft and ashes?"

"Wal, I swan, if that ain't rather queer. And you made it all out of your head naow?" asked the Yankee, looking at the diminutive inventor before him.

"No, I had to use a good deal of iron," was the reply of the youngster, with a quizzical smile.

"You mean you got up the thing yourself?"

"Yes, sir," was the quiet but proud reply of the boy.

"Jingo and Jerusalem! but your daddy must be fond of you!"

exclaimed the enthusiastic New Englander, scanning him admiringly from head to foot.

"I haven't any father."

"Your mother then."

"I don't know about that."

"Say, you, can't yer tell a feller 'bout it?"

"Not now; I haven't time."

As the steam horse was to rest for the present, he was "put up." The engineer opened several cavities in his legs and breast, and different parts of his body, and examined the machinery, carefully oiling the various portions, and when he had completed, he drew a large oil skin from the wagon, which, being spread out, covered both it and the steam man himself.

# CHAPTER III

## A Genius

Having progressed thus far in our story, or properly having began in the middle, it is now necessary that we should turn back to the proper starting point.

Several years since a widow woman resided in the outskirts of St. Louis, whose name was Brainerd. Her husband had been a mechanic, noted for his ingenuity, but was killed some five years before by the explosion of a steam boiler. He left behind him a son, hump-backed, dwarfed, but with an amiable disposition that made him a favorite with all with whom he came in contact.

If nature afflicts in one direction she frequently makes amends in another direction, and this dwarf, small and misshapen as he was, was gifted with a most wonderful mind. His mechanical ingenuity bordered on the marvelous. When he went to school, he was a general favorite with teachers and pupils. The former loved him for his sweetness of disposition, and his remarkable proficiency in all studies, while the latter based their affection chiefly upon the fact that he never refused to assist any of them at their tasks, while with the pocket-knife which he carried he constructed toys which were their delight. Some of these were so curious and amusing that, had they been secured by letters patent, they would have brought a competency to him and his widowed mother.

But Johnny never thought of patenting them, although the principal support of himself and mother came from one or two patents, which his father had secured upon inventions, not near the equal of his.

There seemed no limit to his inventive powers. He made a locomotive and then a steamboat, perfect in every part, even to the minutest, using nothing but his knife, hammer, and a small chisel. He constructed a clock with his jack-knife, which kept perfect time, and the articles which he made were wonderfully stared at at fairs, and in show windows, while Johnny modestly pegged away at some new idea. He became a master of the art of telegraphy without assistance from anyone using merely a common school philosophy with which to acquire the alphabet. He then made a couple of batteries, ran a line from his window to a neighbor's, insulating it by means of the necks of some bottles, taught the other boy the alphabet, and thus they amused themselves sending messages back and forth.

Thus matters progressed until he was fifteen years of age, when he came home one day, and lay down on the settee by his mother, and gave a great sigh.

"What is the matter?" she inquired.

"I want to make something."

"Why, then, don't you make it?"

"Because I don't know what it shall be; I've fixed up everything I can think of."

"And you are like Alexander, sighing for more worlds to conquer. Is that it?"

"Not exactly, for there is plenty for one to do, if I could only find out what it is."

"Have you ever made a balloon?" The boy laughed.

"You were asking for the cat the other day, and wondering what had become of her. I didn't tell you that the last I saw of her was through the telescope, she being about two miles up in the clouds, and going about fifty miles an hour."

"I thought you looked as though you knew something about her," replied the mother, trying to speak reprovingly, and yet smiling in spite of herself.

"Can't you tell me something to make?" finally asked the boy.

"Yes; there is something I have often thought of, and wonder why it was not made long ago; but you are not smart enough to do it, Johnny."

"Maybe not; but tell me what it is."

"It is a man that shall go by steam!" The boy lay still several minutes without speaking a word and then sprung up. "By George! I'll do it!" And he started out of the room, and was not seen again until night. His mother felt no anxiety. She was pleased; for, when her boy was at work, he was happy, and she knew that he had enough now, to keep him engaged for months to come.

So it proved. He spent several weeks in thought, before he made the first effort toward constructing his greatest success of all. He then enlarged his workshop, and so arranged it, that he would not be in danger of being seen by any curious eyes. He wanted no disturbance while engaged upon this scheme.

From a neighboring foundry, whose proprietor took great interest in the boy, he secured all that he needed. He was allowed full liberty to make what castings he chose, and to construct whatever he wished. And so he began his work.

The great point was to obtain the peculiar motion of a man walking. This secured, the man himself could be easily made, and dressed up in any style required. Finally the boy believed that he had hit upon the true scheme.

So he plied harder than ever, scarcely pausing to take his meals. Finally he got the machine together, fired up, and with feelings somewhat akin to those, of Sir Isaac Newton, when demonstrating the truth or falsity of some of his greatest discoveries, he watched the result.

Soon the legs begin moving up and down, but never a step did they advance! The power was there, sufficient to run a saw-mill, everything seemed to work, but the thing wouldn't go!

The boy was not ready to despair. He seated himself on the bench beside the machine, and keeping up a moderate supply of steam, throwing in bits of wood, and letting in water, when necessary, he carefully watched the movement for several hours.

Occasionally, Johnny walked slowly back and forth, and with his eyes upon the "stately stepping," endeavored to discover the precise nature of that which was lacking in his machine.

At length it came to him. He saw from the first that it was not merely required that the steam man should lift up its feet and put them down again, but there must be a powerful forward impulse at the same moment. This was the single remaining difficulty to be overcome. It required two weeks before Johnny Brainerd succeeded. But it all came clear and unmistakable at last, and in this simple manner:

(Ah! but we cannot be so unjust to the plodding genius as to divulge his secret. Our readers must be content to await the time when the young man sees fit to reveal it himself.)

When the rough figure was fairly in working order, the inventor removed everything from around it, so that it stood alone in the center of his shop. Then he carefully let on steam.

Before he could shut it off, the steam man walked clean through the side of his shop, and fetched up against the corner of the house, with a violence that shook it to its foundation. In considerable trepidation, the youngster dashed forward, shut off steam, and turned it round. As it was too cumbersome for him to manage in any other way, he very cautiously let on steam again, and persuaded it to walk back into the shop, passing through the same orifice through which it had emerged, and came very nigh going out on the opposite side again.

The great thing was now accomplished, and the boy devoted himself to bringing it as near perfection as possible. The principal thing to be feared was its getting out of order, since the slightest disarrangement would be sufficient to stop the progress of the man.

Johnny therefore made it of gigantic size, the body and limbs being no more than "Shells," used as a sort of screen to conceal the working of the engine. This was carefully painted in the manner mentioned in another place, and the machinery was made as strong and durable as it was possible for it to be. It was so constructed as to withstand the severe jolting to which it necessarily would be subjected, and finally was brought as nearly perfect as it was possible to bring a thing not possessing human intelligence.

By suspending the machine so that its feet were clear of the floor, Johnny Brainerd ascertained that under favorable circumstances it could run very nearly sixty miles an hour. It could easily do that, and draw a car connected to it on the railroad, while on a common road it could make thirty miles, the highest rate at which he believed it possible for a wagon to be drawn upon land with any degree of safety.

It was the boy's intention to run at twenty miles an hour, while where everything was safe, he would demonstrate the power of the invention by occasionally making nearly double that.

As it was, he rightly calculated that when it came forth, it would make a great sensation throughout the entire United States.

# CHAPTER IV

## The Trapper and the Artisan

"Hello, younker! what in thunder yer tryin' to make?"

Johnny Brainerd paused and looked up, not a little startled by the strange voice and the rather singular figure which stood before him. It was a hunter in half civilized costume, his pants tucked into his immense boot tops, with revolvers and rifles at his waist, and a general negligent air, which showed that he was at home in whatever part of the world he chose to wander.

He stood with his hand in his pocket, chewing his quid, and complacently viewing the operations of the boy, who was not a little surprised to understand how he obtained entrance into his shop.

"Stopped at the house to ax whar old Washoe Pete keeps his hotel," replied the stranger, rightly surmising the query which was agitating him, "and I cotched a glimpse of yer old machine. Thought I'd come in and see what in blazes it war. Looks to me like a man that's gwine to run by steam."

"That's just what it is," replied the boy, seeing there was no use in attempting to conceal the truth from the man.

"Will it do it?"

"Yes, sir."

"Don't think you mean to lie, younker, but I don't believe any such stuff as that."

"It don't make any difference to me whether you believe me or not," was the quiet reply of the boy; "but if you will come inside and shut the door, and let me fasten it, so that there will be no danger of our being disturbed, I will soon show you."

These two personages, so unlike in almost every respect, had taken quite a fancy to each other. The strong, hardy, bronzed trapper, powerful in all that goes to make up the physical man, looked upon the pale, sweet-faced boy, with his misshapen body, as an affectionate father would look upon an afflicted child.

On the other hand, the brusque, outspoken manner of the hunter pleased the appreciative mind of the boy, who saw much to admire, both in his appearance and manner.

"I don't s'pose yer know me," said the stranger, as he stepped inside and allowed the boy to secure the door behind him.

"I never saw you before."

"I am Baldy Bicknell, though I ginerally go by the name of 'Baldy.'"

"That's rather an odd name."

"Yas; that's the reason."

As he spoke, the stranger removed his hat and displayed his clean-shaven pate.

"Yer don't understand that, eh? That 'ere means I had my ha'r lifted ten years ago. The Sioux war the skunks that done it. After they took my top-knot off. It had grow'd on ag'in and that's why they call me Baldy."

In the mean time the door had been closed, and all secured. The hat of the steam man emptied its smoke and steam into a section of stove-pipe, which led into the chimney, so that no suspicion of anything unusual could disturb the passers-by in the street.

"You see it won't do to let him walk here, for when I tried it first, he went straight through the side of the house; but you can tell by the way in which he moves his legs, whether he is able to walk or not."

"That's the way we ginerally gits the p'ints of an animal," returned Baldy, with great complaisance, as he seated himself upon a bench to watch the performance.

It required the boy but a short time to generate a sufficient quantity of steam to set the legs going at a terrific rate, varying the proceedings by letting some of the vapor through the whistle which composed the steam man's nose.

Baldy Bicknell stood for some minutes with a surprise too great to allow him to speak. Wonderful as was the mechanism, yet the boy who had constructed it was still more worthy of wonder. When the steam had given out, the hunter placed his big hand upon the head of the little fellow, and said:

"You'se a mighty smart chap, that be you. Did anybody help you make that?"

"No; I believe not."

"What'll you take for it?"

"I never thought of selling it."

"Wal, think of it now."

"What do you want to do with it?"

"Thar's three of us goin' out to hunt fur gold, and that's jist the thing to keep the Injins back an' scart. I've been out thar afore, and know what's the matter with the darned skunks. So, tell me how much money will buy it."

"I would rather not sell it," said Johnny, after a few minutes' further thought. "It has taken me a great while to finish it, and I would rather not part with it, for the present, at least."

"But, skin me, younker, I want to buy it! I'll give you a thousand dollars fur it, slap down."

Although much less than the machine was really worth, yet it was a large offer, and the boy hesitated for a moment. But it was only for a moment, when he decidedly shook his head.

"I wish you wouldn't ask me, for I don't want to sell it, until I have had it some time. Besides, it isn't finished yet."

"It ain't," exclaimed Baldy, in surprise. "Why, it works, what more do you want?"

"I've got to make a wagon to run behind it."

"That's it, eh? I thought you war goin' to ride on its back. How much will it draw?"

"As much as four horses, and as fast as they can run."

The hunter was half wild with excitement. The boy's delight was never equal to one-half of his.

"Skulp me ag'in, ef that don't beat all! It's jest the thing for the West; we'll walk through the Injins in the tallest kind of style, and skear 'em beautiful. How long afore you'll have it done?"

"It will take a month longer, at least."

Baldy stood a few minutes in thought.

"See here, younker, we're on our way to the "diggin's," and spect to be thar all summer. Ef the red-skins git any ways troublesome, I'm comin' back arter this y'ar covey. Ef yer don't want to sell him, yer needn't. Ef I bought him, it ain't likely I'd run him long afore I'd bust his b'iler, or blow my own head off."

"Just what I thought when you were trying to persuade me to sell it," interrupted the boy.

"Then, if he got the cramp in any of his legs, I wouldn't know how to tie it up ag'in, and thar we'd be."

"I am glad to see you take such a sensible view of it," smiled Johnny.

"So, I'm goin' on West, as I said, with two fools besides myself, and we're goin' to stay thar till yer get this old thing finished; and then I'm comin' after you to take a ride out thar."

"That would suit me very well," replied the boy, his face lighting up with more pleasure than he had shown. "I would be very glad to make a trip on the prairies."

"Wal, look fur me in about six weeks."

And with this parting, the hunter was let out the door, and disappeared, while Johnny resumed his work.

That day saw the steam man completed, so far as it was possible. He was painted up, and every improvement made that the extraordinarily keen mind of the boy could suggest. When he stood one side, and witnessed the noiseless but powerful workings of the enormous legs, he could not see that anything more could be desired.

It now remained for him to complete the wagon, and he began at once.

It would have been a much easier matter for him to have secured an ordinary carriage or wagon, and alter it to suit himself; but this was not in accordance with the genius of the boy. No contrivance could really suit him unless he made it himself. He had his own ideas, which no one else could work out to his satisfaction.

It is unnecessary to say that the vehicle was made very strong and durable.

This was the first great requisite. In some respects it resembled the ordinary express wagons, except that it was considerably smaller.

It had heavy springs, and a canvas covering, with sufficient, as we have shown in another place, to cover the man also, when necessary.

This was arranged to carry the wood, a reserve of water, and the necessary tools to repair it, when any portion of the machinery should become disarranged.

English coal could be carried to last for two days, and enough wood to keep steam going for twenty-four hours. When the reserve tank in the bottom of the wagon was also filled, the water would last nearly as long.

When these contingencies were all provided against, the six weeks mentioned by the hunter were gone, and Johnny Brainerd found himself rather longing for his presence again.

# CHAPTER V

## On the Yellowstone

B aldy Bicknell was a hunter and trapper who, at the time we bring him to the notice of the reader, had spent something over ten years among the mountains and prairies of the West.

He was a brave, skillful hunter, who had been engaged in many desperate affrays with the red-skins, and who, in addition to the loss of the hair upon the crown of his head, bore many other mementos on his person of the wild and dangerous life that he had led.

Like most of his class, he was a restless being, constantly flitting back and forth between the frontier towns and the western wilds. He never went further east than St. Louis, while his wanderings, on more than one occasion, had led him beyond the Rocky Mountains.

One autumn he reached the Yellowstone, near the head of navigation, just as a small trading propeller was descending the stream. As much from the novelty of the thing, as anything else, he rode on board, with his horse, with the intention of completing his journey east by water.

On board the steamer he first met Ethan Hopkins and Mickey McSquizzle, who had spent ten years in California, in a vain hunt for gold, and were now returning to their homes, thoroughly disgusted with the country, its inhabitants and mineral resources.

Baldy was attracted to them by their peculiarities of manner; but it is not probable that anything further would have resulted from this accidental meeting, but for a most startling and unforeseen occurrence.

While still in the upper waters of the Yellowstone, the steamer exploded her boiler, making a complete wreck of the boat and its contents. The hunter, with the others, was thrown into the water, but was so bruised and injured that he found it impossible to swim, and he would assuredly have been drowned but for the timely assistance of his two acquaintances.

Neither the Yankee nor Irishman were hurt in the least, and both falling near the trapper, they instantly perceived his help-lessness and came to his rescue. Both were excellent swimmers, and had no difficulty in saving him.

"Do ye rist aisy!" said Mickey, as he saw the hunter's face con-torted with pain, as he vainly struggled in the water, "and it's ourselves that'll take the good care of yees jist."

"Stop yer confounded floundering," admonished Hopkins; "it won't do no good, and there ain't no necessity for it."

One of them took the arm upon one side, and the other the same upon the opposite side, and struck out for the shore. The poor trapper realized his dire extremity, and remained motion-less while they towed him along.

"Aisy jist—aisy now!" admonished Mickey: "ye're in a bad fix; but by the blessin' of Heaven we'll do the fair thing wid yees. We understand the science of swimmin', and—"

At that moment some drowning wretch caught the foot of the Irishman, and he was instantly drawn under water, out of sight.

Neither Hopkins nor Baldy lost presence of mind in this fear-ful moment, but continued their progress toward shore, as though nothing of the kind had happened.

As for the Irishman, his situation for the time was exceedingly critical. The man who had clutched his foot did so with the grasp of a drowning man; in their struggle both went to the bottom of the river together. Here, by a furious effort, Mickey shook him free, and coming to the surface, struck out again for the suffering hunter.

"It is sorry I am that I was compelled to leave yees behind," he muttered, glancing over his shoulder in search of the poor fellow from whom he had just freed himself; "but yees are past helpin', and so it's maeself that must attend to the poor gentleman ahead."

Striking powerfully out, he soon came beside his friends again and took the drooping arm of Baldy Bicknell.

"Be yees sufferin' to a great extent?" inquired the kind-hearted Irishman, looking at the white face of the silent hunter.

"Got a purty good whack over the back," he replied, between his compressed lips, as he forced back all expression of pain.

"Ye'll be aisier when we fotch ye to the land, as me uncle observed whin he hauled the big fish ashore that was thrashing his line to pieces jist."

"Twon't take you long to git over it," added Hopkins, anxious to give his grain of consolation; "you look, now, like quite a healthy young man."

The current was quite rapid, and it was no light labor to tow the helpless hunter ashore; but the two friends succeeded, and at length drew him out upon the land and stretched him upon the sward.

The exertion of keeping their charge afloat, and breasting the current at the same time, carried them a considerable distance downstream, and they landed perhaps an eighth of a mile below where the main body of shivering wretches were congregated.

"Do yees feel aisy?" inquired Mickey, when the hunter had been laid upon the grass, beneath some overhanging bushes.

"Yes, I'll soon git over it but woofh! that thar war a whack of the biggest kind I got. It has made me powerful weak."

"What might it have been naow!" inquired Hopkins.

"Can't say, fust thing I know'd, I didn't know nothin', remember suthin' took me back the head, and the next thing I kerwholloped in the water."

The three men had lost everything except what was on their bodies when the catastrophe occurred. Their horses were gone, and they hadn't a gun between them; nothing but two revolvers, and about a half dozen charges for each.

Of the twenty odd who were upon the steamer at the time of the explosion, nearly one-half were killed; they sinking to the bottom almost as suddenly as the wrecked steamer, of which not a single trace now remained.

The survivors made their way to land, reaching it a short distance below their starting-point, and here they assembled, to commiserate with each other upon their hapless lot and determine how they were to reach home.

Our three friends had remained upon shore about half an

hour, the two waiting for the third to recover, when the latter raised himself upon his elbow in the attitude of listening. At the same time he waved his hand for the others to hold their peace.

A moment later he said:

"I hear Injins."

"Begorrah! where bees the same?" demanded Mickey, starting to his feet, while Ethan gazed alarmedly about.

"Jist take a squint up the river, and tell me ef they ain't pitchin' into the poor critters thar."

Through the sheltering trees and undergrowth, which partly protected them, the two men gazed up-stream. To their horror, they saw fully fifty Indians massacring the survivors of the wreck, whooping, screeching and yelling like demons, while their poor victims were vainly endeavoring to escape them.

"Begorrah, now, but that looks bad!" exclaimed the Irishman. "Be the same towken, what is it that we can do?"

"Jerusalem! They'll be sure to pay us a visit. I'll be gumtued if they won't," added the Yankee, in some trepidation, as he cowered down again by the side of the hunter, and said to him in a lower voice:

"The worst of it is, we haven't got a gun atwixt us. Of course we shall stick by you if we have to lose our heads fur it. But don't you think they'll pay us a visit?"

"Like 'noughtin',' was the indifferent reply of the hunter, as he laid his head back again, as if tired of listening to the tumult.

"Can't we do anything to get you out of danger!"

"Can't see that you kin; you two fellers have done me a good turn in gittin' me ashore, so jist leave me yere, and it don't make no difference about me one way or t'other. Ef I hear 'em comin' I'll jist roll into the water and go under in that style."

"May the Howly Vargin niver smile upon us if we dissart you in this extremity," was the reply of the fervent-hearted Irishman.

"And by the jumpin' jingo! if we was consarnedly mean enough to do it, there ain't no need of it."

As the Yankee spoke, he ran down to the river, and walking out a short distance, caught a log drifting by and drew it in.

"Naow, Mr. Baldy, or Mr. Bicknell, as you call yourself, we'll all three git hold of that and float down the river till we git beyond fear of the savages."

The plan was a good one, and the hunter so expressed himself. With some help he managed to crawl to the river bank, where one arm was placed over the log, in such a manner that he could easily float, without any danger of sinking.

"Keep as close to shore as you kin," he said, as they were about shoving off.

"We can go faster in the middle," said Hopkins.

"But the reds'll see us, and it'll be all up then."

This was the warning of prudence, and it was heeded.

# CHAPTER VI

## The Miners

It was late in the afternoon when the explosion occurred, and it was just beginning to grow dark when the three friends began drifting down the Yellowstone.

This fact was greatly in their favor, although there remained an hour or two of great danger, in case the Indians made any search for them. In case of discovery, there was hardly an earthly chance for escape.

The log or raft, as it might be termed, had floated very quietly down-stream for about half an hour, when the wonderfully acute ears of the trapper detected danger.

"Thar be some of the skunks that are creep-in "long shore," said he; "you'd better run in under this yar tree and hold fast awhile."

The warning was heeded. Just below them, the luxuriant branches of an oak, dipped in the current, formed an impenetrable screen. As the log, guided thither, floated beneath this, Mickey and Ethan both caught hold of the branches and held themselves motionless.

"Now wait till it's dark, and then thar'll be no fear of the varmints," added the trapper.

"Sh! I haars sumfin'!" whispered the Irishman.

"What is it?" asked Ethan.

"How does I know till yees kaaps still?"

"It's the reds goin' long the banks," said the trapper.

The words were yet in his mouth, when the voice of one Indian was heard calling to another. Neither Mickey nor Ethan had the remotest idea of the meaning of the words uttered, but the trapper told them that they were inquiring of each other whether anything had been discovered of more fugitives. The answer being in the negative, our friends considered their present position safe.

When it was fairly dark, and nothing more was seen or heard of the Indians, the raft was permitted to float free, and they drifted with the current. They kept the river until daylight, when, having been in the water so long, they concluded it best to land and rest themselves. By the aid of their revolvers they succeeded in kindling a fire, the warmth of which proved exceedingly grateful to all.

They would have had a very rough time had they not encountered a party of hunters who accompanied them to St. Louis, where the trapper had friends, and where, also, he had a good sum of money in the bank.

Here Baldy remained all winter, before he entirely recovered from the hurt which he received during the explosion and sinking of the steamer. When the Irishman and Yankee were about to depart, he asked them where they were going.

"I'm goin' home in Connecticut and goin' to work on the farm, and that's where I'm goin' to stay. I was a fool ever to leave it for this confounded place. I could live decent put there, and that's more than I can do in this blamed country."

"And I shall go back to work on the Erie railroad, at thirty-siven cents a day and boord myself," replied the Irishman.

"If yer were sartin of findin' all the gold yor want, would yer go back to Califony?"

"Arrah. Now, what are yees talkin' about?" asked McSquizzle, somewhat impatiently. "What is the good of talkin'?"

"I didn't ax yer to fool with yer," replied the trapper, "thar's a place that I know away out West, that I call Wolf Ravine, whar thar's enough gold to make both of yer richer than yer ever war afore, and then leave some for yer children."

"Jerusalem! but you're a lucky dog!" exclaimed Ethan Hopkins, not daring to hope that he would reveal the place. "Why don't you dig it up naow, yourself?"

"I only found it a month ago, and I made a purty good haul of it, as it was. When that old boss of mine went down with

the steamer, he carried a powerful heft of gold with him, and if anybody finds his carcass, it'll be the most vallyable one they ever come across."

"Jingo! if I'd know'd that, I'd taken a hunt for him myself."

"Howsumever, that's neither yar nor thar. You both done me a good turn when I got into trouble on the river, and I mud' up my mind to do what I could toward payin' it back the first chance I got. I didn't say nothin' of it when we was on our way, 'cause I was afeard it would make you too crazy to go back ag'in: but if you'll come back this way next spring I'll make the trip with you."

"Why not go naow?" eagerly inquired Hopkins.

"It's too late in the season. I don't want to be thar when thar's too much snow onto the ground, and then I must stay yar till I git well over that whack I got on the boat."

It is hardly necessary to say that the offer of the kind-hearted trapper was accepted with the utmost enthusiasm. Mickey and Ethan were more anxious to go out upon the prairies than they had been a year and a half before, when they started so full of life and hope for that vast wilderness, and had come back with such discouragement and disgust.

It was arranged that as soon as the succeeding spring had fairly set in, they would set out on their return for St. Louis, where the trapper would meet and accompany them to the wonderful gold region of which he had spoken.

Before continuing their journey homeward, Baldy presented each with a complete outfit, paid their passage to their homes, and gave them a snug sum over. Like the Indian, he never could forget a kindness shown him, nor do too great a favor to those who had so signally benefited him.

So the separation took place again; and, on the following spring Mickey and Ethan appeared in St. Louis, where they had no difficulty in finding their old friend, the trapper.

He had recovered entirely from his prostrating blow, and was expecting them, anxious and glad to join in the promised search for gold. As the fair weather had really begun, there was no time lost in unnecessary delay. The purse of Baldy Bicknell was deep, and he had not the common habit of intoxication, which takes so much substance from a man. He purchased a horse and accouterments for each of his friends; and, before they started westward, saw that nothing at all was lacking in their outfit.

Three weeks later the men drew rein in a sort of valley, very deep but not very wide. It was on the edge of an immense prairie, while a river of considerable size flowed by the rear, and by a curious circuit found its way into the lower portion of the ravine, dashing and roaring forward in a furious canyon.

The edge and interior of the ravine was lined with immense boulders and rocks, while large and stunted trees seemed to grow everywhere.

"Yar's what I call Wolf Ravine," said Baldy when they had spent some time in looking about them.

"And be the same towken, where is the goold?" inquired Mickey.

"Yes, that there is what I call the important question," added Ethan.

"That it is, of the greatest account, as me grandmither observed, whin she fell off the staaple, and axed whether her pipe was broke."

"It's in thar," was the reply of the hunter, as he pointed to the wildest-looking portion of the ravine.

"Let's geit it then."

"Thar be some other things that have got to be looked after first," was the reply, "and we've got to find a place to stow ourselves away."

This was a matter of considerable difficulty: but they succeeded at last in discovering a retreat in the rocks, where they were secure from any attack, no matter by how formidable a number made.

After this, they hunted up a grazing place for their animals, which were turned loose.

They soon found that the trapper had not deceived them. There was an unusually rich deposit of gold in one portion of the ravine, and the men fell to work with a will, conscious that they would reap a rich reward for their labor.

The name, Wolf Ravine, had been given to it by the trapper, because on his first discovery of it he had shot a large mountain wolf that was clambering up the side; but none others were seen afterward.

But there was one serious drawback to this brilliant prospect of wealth. Indians of the most treacherous and implacable kind were all around them, and were by no means disposed to let them alone.

On the second day after their labor, a horde of them came screeching down upon them; and had it not been for the safe retreat, which the trapper's foresight had secured, all three would have been massacred.

As it was, they had a severe fight, and were penned up for the better part of two days, by which time they had slain too many of their enemies that the remaining ones were glad to withdraw.

But when the trapper stole out on a visit to his horses he found that everyone had been completely riddled by balls. The treacherous dogs had taken every means of revenge at hand.

"Skin me fur a skunk, but we've stood this long as we ought to!" exclaimed Baldy Bicknell, when he returned. "You take care of yourselves till I come back again!"

With which speech he slung his rifle over his shoulder and started for St. Louis.

# CHAPTER VII

# The Steam Man on His Travels

Young Brainerd had a mortal fear that the existence of the steam man would be discovered by some outsider, then a large crowd would probably collect around his house, and his friends would insist on a display of the powers of the extraordinary mechanism.

But there was no one in the secret except his mother, and there was no danger of her revealing it. So the boy experimented with his invention until there was nothing more left for him to do, except to sit and watch its workings.

Finally, when he began to wonder at the prolonged delay of the trapper, who had visited him some weeks before, he made his appearance as suddenly as if he had risen from the ground, with the inquiry:

"Have you got that thundering old thing ready?"

"Yes: he has been ready for a week, and waiting."

"Wal, start her out then, fur I'm in a hurry."

"You will have to wait awhile, for we can't get ready under half a day."

It was the hunter's supposition that the boy was going to start the man right off up street, and then toward the West; but he speedily revealed a far different plan.

It was to box up the man and take it to Independence by steamboat. At that place they would take it out upon the prairie, set it up and start it off, without any fear of disturbance from the crowds which usually collect at such places, as they could speedily run away from them.

When the plan was explained to Baldy, he fully endorsed it,

and the labor was begun at once. The legs of the steam man being doubled up, they were able to get it in a box, which gave it the appearance of an immense piano under transportation. This, with considerable difficulty, was transported to the wharf, where, with much grumbling upon the part of the men, it was placed on board the steamboat, quickly followed by the wagon and the few necessary tools.

The boy then bade his mother good-by, and she, suspecting he would be gone but a short time, said farewell to him, with little of the regret she would otherwise have felt, and a few hours later the party were steaming rapidly up the "Mad Missouri."

Nothing worthy of notice occurred on the passage, and they reached Independence in safety. They secured a landing somewhat above the town, on the western side, where they had little fear of disturbance.

Here the extraordinary foresight and skill of the boy was manifest, for, despite the immense size of the steam man, it was so put together that they were able to load it upon the wagon, and the two, without any other assistance, were able to drag it out upon the prairie.

"You see, it may break down entirely," remarked young Brainerd, "and then we can load it on the wagon and drag it along."

"That must be a powerful strong wagon to carry such a big baby in it, as that."

"So it is; it will hold five times the weight without being hurt in the least."

It was early in the forenoon when they drew it out upon the prairie in this manner, and began putting it together. It certainly had a grotesque and fearful look when it was stripped of all its bandages, and stood before them in all its naked majesty.

It had been so securely and carefully put away, that it was found uninjured in the least. The trapper could not avoid laughing when the boy clambered as nimbly up its shoulder as another Gulliver, and made a minute examination of every portion of the machinery.

While thus employed, Baldy took the shafts of the wagon, and trotted to a farm-house, which he spied in the distance, where he loaded it down with wood and filled the tank with water. By the time he returned, Johnny had everything in readiness, and they immediately began "firing up."

In this they bore quite a resemblance to the modern steam fire engines, acquiring a head of steam with remarkable quickness. As the boy had never yet given the man such an opportunity to stretch his legs as he was now about to do, he watched its motions with considerable anxiety.

Everything was secured in the most careful manner, a goodly quantity of fuel piled on, the boiler filled with water, and they patiently waited the generation of a sufficient head of steam.

"Is it all good prairie land in that direction?" inquired the boy, pointing to the West.

"Thar's all yer kin want."

"Then we'll start. Look out!"

Despite the warning thus kindly given, the steam man started with a sudden jerk, that both of them came near being thrown out of the wagon.

The prairie was quite level and hard, so that everything was favorable, and the wagon went bounding over the ground at a rate so fast that both the occupants were considerably frightened, and the boy quickly brought it down to a more moderate trot.

This speed soon became monotonous, and as it ran so evenly, Baldy said:

"Let her go, younker, and show us what she can do."

The rod controlling the valve was given a slight pull, and away they went, coursing like a locomotive over the prairies, the wheels spinning round at a tremendous rate, while the extraordinary speed caused the wind thus created almost to lift the caps from their heads, and a slight swell in the prairie sent the wagon up with a bound that threatened to unseat them both.

It worked splendidly. The black smoke puffed rapidly from the top of the hat, and the machinery worked so smoothly that there was scarcely a click heard. The huge spiked feet came lightly to the ground, and were lifted but a short distance from it, and their long sweep and rapid movement showed unmistakably that the steam man was going at a pace which might well defy anything that had yet swept the prairies.

As there was no little risk in running at this speed, and as young Brainerd had not yet become accustomed to controlling it, he slackened the rate again, so that it sank to an easy gliding motion, equal to the rapid trot of an ordinary horse.

Fully ten minutes were passed in this manner, when steam was entirely shut off, whereupon the giant came to such a sudden halt that both were thrown violently forward and bruised somewhat.

"Skulp me! but don't stop quite so sudden like," said the hunter. "It's a little unhandy fur me to hold up so quick!"

"I'll soon learn to manage it," replied Johnny. "I see it won't do to shut off all at once."

Descending from his perch, he examined every portion of the engine. Several parts were found heated, and the fuel was getting low. The water in the boiler, however, was just right, the engineer having been able to control that from his seat in the wagon.

Throwing in a lot of wood, they remounted to their perch and started forward again. There was an abundance of steam, and the boy readily acquired such a familiarity with the working of his man, that he controlled it with all the skill of an experienced engineer.

The speed was slackened, then increased. It stopped and then started forward again with all the ease and celerity that it could have done if really human, while it showed a reserve of power and velocity capable of performing wonders, if necessary.

As yet they had seen nothing of any travelers. They were quite anxious to come across some, that they might show them what they were capable of doing.

"There must be some passing over the plains," remarked Johnny, when they had passed some thirty or forty miles.

"Plenty of 'em; but we've got out of the track of 'em. If you'll turn off summat to the left, we'll run foul of 'em afore dark."

The boy did as directed, and the rattling pace was kept up for several hours. When it was noon they helped themselves to a portion of the food which they brought with them, without checking their progress in the least. True, while the boy was eating, he kept one eye on the giant who was going at such rapid strides; but that gentleman continued his progress in an unexceptionable manner, and needed no attention.

When the afternoon was mostly gone, Baldy declared that they had gone the better part of a hundred miles.

The boy could hardly credit it at first; but, when he recalled that they had scarcely paused for seven hours, and had gone a portion of the distance at a very high rate, he saw that his friend was not far out of the way.

It lacked yet several hours of dusk, when the trapper exclaimed:

"Yonder is an emigrant train, now make for 'em!"

# CHAPTER VIII

# Indians

The steam man was headed straight toward the emigrant train, and advanced at a speed which rapidly came up with it.

They could see, while yet a considerable distance away, that they had attracted notice, and the emigrants had paused and were surveying them with a wonder which it would be difficult to express.

It is said that when Robert Fulton's first steamboat ascended the Hudson, it created a consternation and terror such as had never before been known, many believing that it was the harbinger of the final destruction of the world.

Of course, at this late day, no such excitement can be created by any human invention, but the sight of a creature speeding over the country, impelled by steam, and bearing such a grotesque resemblance to a gigantic man, could not but startle all who should see it for the first time.

The steam man advanced at a rate which was quite moderate, until within a quarter of a mile of the astonished train, when the boy let on a full head of steam and instantly bounded forward like a meteor. As it came opposite the amazed company, the whistle was pulled, and it gave forth a shriek hideous enough to set a man crazy.

The horses and animals of the emigrant train could be seen rearing and plunging, while the men stood too appalled to do anything except gaze in stupid and speechless amazement.

There were one or two, however, who had sense enough to perceive that there was nothing at all very supernatural about it, and they shouted to them to halt; but our two friends concluded it was not desirable to have any company, and they only slackened their speed, without halting.

But there was one of the emigrants who determined to know something more about it and, mounting his horse, he started after it on a full run. The trapper did not perceive him until he had approached quite close, when they again put on a full head of steam, and they went bounding forward at a rate which threatened to tear them to pieces.

But the keen perception of the boy had detected what they were able to do without real risk: and, without putting his invention to its very best, he kept up a speed which steadily drew them away from their pursuer, who finally became discouraged, checked his animal, and turned round and rode back to his friends, a not much wiser man.

This performance gave our friends great delight. It showed them that they were really the owners of a prize whose value was incalculable.

"Ef the old thing will only last," said Baldy, when they had sunk down to a moderate trot again.

"What's to binder?"

"Dunno; yer oughter be able to tell. But these new-fangled things generally go well at first, and then, afore yer know it, they bust all to blazes."

"No fear of this. I made this fellow so big that there is plenty of room to have everything strong and give it a chance to work."

"Wal, you're the smartest feller I ever seen, big or little. Whoever heard of a man going by steam?"

"I have, often; but I never saw it. I expect when I go back to make steam horses."

"And birds, I s'pose?"

"Perhaps so; it will take some time to get such things in shape, but I hope to do it after awhile."

"Skulp me! but thar must be some things that you can't do, and I think you've mentioned 'em.

"Perhaps so," was the quiet reply. "When you git through with this Western trip, what are you goin' to do with this old feller?"

"I don't know. I may sell him, if anybody wants him."

"No fear of that; I'll take him off your hands, and give you a good price for him."

"What good will he do you?"

"Why, you can make more money with him than Barnum ever did with his Woolly Home."

"How so?" inquired the boy, with great simplicity.

"Take him through the country and show him to the people. I tell yer they'd run after such things. Get out yer pictures of him, and the folks would break thar necks to see him. I tell yer, thar's a fortune thar!"

The trapper spoke emphatically like one who knows.

As it was growing dusk, they deemed it best to look for some camping-place. There was considerable danger in running at night, as there was no moon, and they might run into some gully or ravine and dislocate or wrench some portion of their machinery, which might result in an irreparable catastrophe.

Before it was fairly dark they headed toward a small clump of trees, where everything looked favorable.

"You see we must find a place where there is plenty water and fuel, for we need both," remarked the boy.

"Thar's plenty of wood, as yer see with yer eyes," replied Baldy, "and when trees look as keen as that, thar's purty sure sign thar's water not fur off."

"That's all we want," was the observation of the engineer as he headed toward the point indicated.

Things were growing quite indistinct, when the steam man gave its last puff, and came to rest in the margin of the grove. The fires were instantly drawn, and everything was put in as good shape as possible, by the boy, while the trapper made a tour of examination through the grove. He came back with the report that everything was as they wished.

"Thar's a big stream of water runnin' right through the middle, and yer can see the wood fur yourself."

"Any signs of Indians?" asked the boy, in a low voice, as if fearful of being overheard. "Dunno; it's too dark to tell."

"If it's dangerous here, we had better go on."

"Yer ain't much used to this part the world. You may keep powerful easy till mornin'."

As they could not feel certain whether in danger or not, it was the part of prudence to believe that some peril threatened them. Accordingly they ate their evening meal in silence, and curled up in the bottom of their wagon, first taking the precaution to fill their tank with water, and placing a portion of wood and kindlings in the bowels of the steam man, so that in case of danger, they would be able to leave at a short notice.

Johnny Brainerd was soon sound asleep, and the trapper followed, but it was with that light, restless slumber which is disturbed by the slightest noise.

So it came about that, but a few hours had passed, when he was aroused by some slight disturbance in the grove. Raising his head he endeavored to peer into the darkness, but he could detect nothing.

But he was certain that something was there, and he gently aroused the boy beside him.

"What is it?" queried the latter in a whisper, but fully wide-awake.

"I think thar ar Ingins among the trees."

"Good heavens! what shall we do?"

"Keep still and don't git skeart! sh!" At this juncture he heard a slight noise, and cautiously raising his head, he caught the outlines of an Indian, in a crouching position, stealing along in front of the wagon, as though examining the curious contrivance. He undoubtedly was greatly puzzled, but he remained only a few minutes, when he withdrew as silently as he had come.

"Stay yer, while I take a look around!" whispered Baldy, as he slid softly out the wagon, while the boy did the same, waiting; until sure that the trapper would not see him.

Baldy spent a half-hour in making his reconnaissance. The result of it was that he found there were fully twenty Indians, thoroughly wide-awake, who were moving stealthily through the grove.

When he came back, it was with the conviction that their only safety lay in getting away without delay.

"We've got to learn," said he, "how long it will take yer to git up steam, youngster?"

"There is a full head on now. I fired up the minute you left the wagon."

"Good!" exclaimed Baldy, who in his excitement did not observe that the steam man was seething, and apparently ready to explode with the tremendous power pent up in its vitals.

# CHAPTER IX

## The Steam Man as a Hunter

At this juncture the trapper whispered that the Indians were again stealing around them. Johnny's first proceeding was to pull the whistle wide open, awaking the stillness of the night by a hideous, prolonged screech.

Then, letting on the steam, the man made a bound forward, and the next moment was careering over the prairie like a demon of darkness, its horrid whistle giving forth almost one continual yell, such as no American Indian has ever been able to imitate.

When they had gone a few hundred yards, Johnny again slackened the speed, for there was great risk in going at this tremendous rate, where all was entire blank darkness, and there was no telling into what danger they might run. At the speed at which they were going they would have bounded into a river before they could have checked themselves.

"Yer furgot one thing," said Baldy, when they had considerably moderated their gait, and were using great caution.

"What is that?"

"Yer oughter had a lamp in front, so we could travel at night, jist as well as day."

"You are right; I don't see how I came to forget that. We could have frightened the Indians more completely, and there would have been some consolation in traveling at such a time."

"Is it too late yet?"

"Couldn't do it without going back to St. Louis."

"Thunderation! I didn't mean that. Go ahead."

"Such a lamp or head-light as the locomotives use would cost several hundred dollars, although I could have made one nearly as good for much less. Such a thing in the center of a man's fore-head, and the whistle at the end of his nose, would give him quite an impressive appearance."

"Yer must do it, too, some day My God!"

The boy instantly checked their progress, as the trapper uttered his exclamation; but quickly as it was done, it was none too soon, for another long step and the steam man would have gone down an embankment, twenty feet high, into a roaring river at the base. As it was, both made rather a hurried leap to the ground, and ran to the front to see whether there was not danger of his going down.

But fortunately he stood firm.

"I declare that was a narrow escape!" exclaimed the boy as he gazed down the cavernous darkness, looking doubly frightful in the gloom of the night.

"Skulp me if that wouldn't have been almost as bad as staying among the red-skins," replied the trapper. "How are we goin' to get him out of this?"

"We've got to shove him back ourselves."

"Can't we reverse him?"

"No; he isn't gotten up on that principle."

By great labor they managed to make him retrograde a few steps, so that he could be made to shy enough to leave the dangerous vicinity, and once more started upon the broad firm prairie.

"Do you suppose these Indians are following us?" inquired the boy.

"No fear of it."

"Then we may as well stay here."

The fires were drawn again, everything made right, and the two disposed themselves again for spending the night in slumber.

No disturbance occurred, and both slept roundly until broad daylight. The trapper's first proceeding upon awakening was to scan the prairie in every direction in quest of danger.

He was not a little amused to see a dozen or so mounted Indians about a third of a mile to the west. They had reined up on the plain, and were evidently scanning the strange object, with a great deal of wonder, mixed with some fear.

"Do you think they will attack us?" inquired the boy, who

could not suppress his trepidation at the sight of the warlike savages, on their gayly-caparisoned horses, drawn up in such startling array.

"Ef thar war any danger of that, we could stop 'em by 'tacking 'em."

"Jest fire up and start toward 'em, and see how quick they will scatter." The advice was acted upon on the instant, although it was with no little misgiving on the part of the engineer.

All the time that the "firing-up" process was under way the savages sat as motionless as statues upon their horses. Had they understood the real nature of the "animal," it cannot be supposed that they would have hesitated for a moment to charge down upon it and demolish it entirely.

But it was a terra incognita, clothed with a terror such as no array of enemies could wear, and they preferred to keep at a goodly distance from it.

"Now, suppose they do not run?" remarked Johnny, rather doubtingly, as he hesitated whether to start ahead or not.

"What if they don't? Can't we run another way? But yer needn't fear. Jist try it on."

Steam was let on as rapidly as possible, and the momentum gathering quickly, it was soon speeding over the prairie at a tremendous rate, straight toward the savages.

The latter remained motionless a few moments, before they realized that it was coming after them, and then, wheeling about, they ran as though all the legions of darkness were after them.

"Shall I keep it up?" shouted Johnny in the ear of the hunter.

"Yas; give 'em such a skear that they won't be able to git over it ag'in in all thar lives."

There is some fun in chasing a foe, when you know that he is really afraid of you, and will keep running without any thought of turning at bay, and the dwarf put the steam man to the very highest notch of speed that was safe, even at the slight risk of throwing both the occupants out.

The prairie was harder and nearer level than any over which they had passed since starting, so that nothing was in the way of preventing the richest kind of sport.

"Are we gaining?" inquired Johnny, his eyes glowing with excitement.

"Gaining? Thar never was a red-skin that had such a chase in all the world. Ef they don't git out the way mighty soon, we'll run over 'em all."

They were, in truth, rapidly overhauling the red-skins, who were about as much terrified as it was possible for a mortal to be, and still live.

To increase their fears, the boy kept up a constant shrieking of his whistle. If there had been any other contrivance or means at his command, it is possible the redskins would have tumbled off their horses and died; for they were bearing almost all the fright, terror and horror that can possibly be concentrated into a single person.

Finding there was no escape by means of the speed of their horses, the Indians sensibly did what the trapper had prophesied they would do at first.

They "scattered," all diverging over the prairie. As it was impossible for the steam man to overtake all of these, of course, this expedient secured the safety of the majority.

Neither Baldy nor the boy were disposed to give up the sport in this manner; so, they singled out a single "noble red-man," who was pursuing nearly the same direction as they were, and they headed straight for him.

The poor wretch, when he saw that he was the object of the monster's pursuit, seemed to become frantic with terror. Rising on his horse's back, he leaned forward until it looked as though there was danger of going over his head altogether. Then, whooping and shrieking to his terrified horse, that was already straining every nerve, he pounded his heels in its sides, vainly urging it to still greater speed.

In the mean time, the steam man was gaining steadily upon him, while to add variety to the scene, Johnny kept up the unearthly shrieking of the nose-whistle of the giant. It was difficult to tell which sounded the most hideously in this strange chase.

The remaining Indians had improved their advantage to the utmost. Fearful that their dreadful enemy might change its mind and single them out, they kept up their tearing light, all regardless of the great extremity to which their companion was reduced, until finally they disappeared in the distance.

A short distance only separated pursuer and pursued, when the latter, realizing that there was no escape in flight, headed toward the river, which was a short distance on the right.

This saved him. When with a howl, horse and rider thundered over the bank and disappeared, the steam man could not follow him. He was compelled to give up the chase and draw off. A few days later, and without further noteworthy incident, the steam man reached Wolf Ravine, being received in the manner narrated at the beginning of this story.

# CHAPTER X

## Wolf Ravine

During the absence of Baldy Bicknell in search of the steam man, neither Mickey nor Ethan had been disturbed by Indians.

They had worked unceasingly in digging the gold mine to which they had gained access through the instrumentality of the trapper. When they had gathered together quite a quantity of the gravel and dirt, with the yellow sand glittering through it, it was carried a short distance to the margin of the river, where it underwent the "washing" process.

While thus engaged, one of them was constantly running up the bank, to make sure that their old enemies did not steal upon them unawares. Once or twice they caught sight of several moving in the distance, but they did not come near enough to molest them, doing nothing more than to keep them on the quiver.

There was one Indian, however, who bestrode a black horse, who haunted them like a phantom. When they glanced over the river, at almost any time, they could see this individual cautiously circling about on his horse, and apparently waiting for a chance to get a shot at his enemies.

"Begorrah, but he loves us, that he does, as the lamb observed when speaking of the wolf," said Mickey, just after he had sent a bullet whistling about their ears.

"Jehosiphat! he loves us too much!" added the Yankee, who had no relish for these stolen shots. "If we ain't keerful, there'll be nuthin' of us left when Baldy comes back, that is, if he comes back at all."

This red-skin on his black horse was so dangerous that he

required constant watching, and the men could perform only half their usual work. It was while Mickey was on the lookout for him that he caught sight of the steam man coming toward him, as we have related in another place.

So long as that personage was kept puffing and tearing round the vicinity, they knew there was no fear of disturbance from the treacherous red-skins, who were so constantly on the alert to avenge themselves for the loss they had suffered in the attack; but it would hardly pay to keep an iron man as sentinel, as the wear and tear in all probability would be too much for him.

After consulting together upon the return of Baldy, and after they had ridden behind the steam man to their heart's content, they decided upon their future course. As the boy, Johnny, had no intention of devoting himself to manual labor, even had he been able, it was agreed that he should take upon himself the part of sentinel, while the others were at work.

In this way it was believed that they could finish within a couple of weeks, bidding good-by to the Indians, and quickly reach the States and give up their dangerous pursuits altogether, whereas, if compelled to do duty themselves as sentinels, their stay would be doubly prolonged.

This arrangement suited the boy very well, who was thereby given opportunity to exercise his steam man by occasional airings over the prairies. To the east and south the plains stretched away till the horizon shut down upon them, as the sky does on the sea. To the west, some twenty odd miles distant, a range of mountains was visible, the peaks being tinged with a faint blue in the distance, while some of the more elevated looked like white conical clouds resting against the clear sky beyond.

From the first, young Brainerd expressed a desire to visit these mountains. There was something in their rugged grandeur which invited a close inspection, and he proposed to the trapper that they should make a hunting excursion in that direction.

"No need of goin' so fur for game," he replied, "takes too much time, and thar's sure to be red-skins."

"But if we go with the steam man we shall frighten them all away," was the reply.

"Yas," laughed Baldy, "and we'll skear the game away too."

"But we can overtake that as we did the poor Indian the other day."

"Not if he takes to the mountains. Leastways yer isn't him that would like to undertake to ride up the mountain behind that old gintle-man."

"Nor I either, but we can leave the wagon when we get to the base of the mountain."

"And give the reds time to come down and run off with yer whole team."

"Do you think there is danger of that?"

"Dunno as thar be, but ef they catched sight of yourself, they'd raise yer ha'r quicker'n lightning."

Seeing that the little fellow was considerably discouraged, Baldy hastened to add:

"Ef you're keerful, younker, and I b'lieve yer generally be, take a ride thar yerself, behind yer jumping-jack, but remember my advice and stick to yer wagon."

Having thus obtained permission of the hunter, Johnny Brainerd, as may well be supposed, did not wait long before availing himself of his privilege.

The weather, which had been threatening toward the latter part of the day, entirely cleared away, and the next morning dawned remarkably clear and beautiful. So the boy announced his intention of making the expected visit, after which, he promised to devote himself entirely to performing the duty of sentinel.

"About what time may we look for you, neow!" asked Ethan, as he was on the point of starting.

"Sometime this afternoon."

"Come in before dark, as me mither used to observe to meself, when I wint out shparkin'," added Mickey.

The boy promised to heed their warnings, and began firing up again. The tank was completely filled with water, and the wagon filled nearly full of wood, so that the two were capable of running the contrivance for the entire day, provided there was no cessation, and that he was on the "go" continually.

Before starting, it was thoroughly oiled through and through, and put in the best possible condition, and then waving them all a pleasant farewell, he steamed gayly toward the mountains.

The ground was admirable, and the steam man traveled better than ever. Like a locomotive, he seemed to have acquired a certain smoothness and steadiness of motion, from the exercise he had already had, and the sharp eye of the boy detected it at once. He saw that he had been very fortunate indeed in constructing his wonderful invention, as it was impossible for any human skill to give it any better movement than it now possessed.

The first three or four miles were passed at a rattling gait, and the boy was sitting on the front of his wagon, dreamily watching the play of the huge engine, when it suddenly paused, and with such abruptness that he was thrown forward from his seat, with violence, falling directly between the legs of the monster, which seemed to stand perfectly motionless, like the intelligent elephant that is fearful of stirring a limb, lest he might crush his master lying beneath him.

The boy knew at once that some accident had happened, and unmindful of the severe scratch he had received, he instantly clambered to his feet, and began examining the machinery, first taking the precaution to give vent to the surplus steam, which was rapidly gathering.

It was some time before he could discover the cause of difficulty, but he finally ascertained that a small bolt had slipped loose, and had caught in such a manner as to check the motion of the engine on the instant.

Fortunately no permanent injury was done, and while he was making matters right, he recollected that in chatting with the trapper as he was on the point of starting, he had begun to screw on the bolt, when his attention had been momentarily diverted, when it escaped his mind altogether, so that he alone was to blame for the accident, which had so narrowly escaped proving a serious one.

Making sure that everything was right, he remounted the wagon, and cautiously resumed his journey, going very slowly at first, so as to watch the play of the engine.

Everything moved with its usual smoothness, and lifting his

gaze he spied three buffaloes, standing with erect heads, staring wonderingly at him.

"If you want a chase you may have it!" exclaimed the boy as he headed toward them.

# CHAPTER XI

## The Steam Man on a Buffalo Hunt

With a wild snort of alarm, the three buffaloes turned tail and dashed over the prairie, with the shrieking steam man in pursuit.

The boy had taken the precaution to bring a rifle with him. When he saw them flee in this terrified manner, the thought came to him at once that he would shoot one of them, and take a portion back to his friends for their supper.

It would be a grand exploit for him, and he would be prouder of its performance than he was of the construction of the wonderful steam man.

The lumbering, rolling gait of the buffaloes was not a very rapid one, and the boy found himself speedily overhauling them without difficulty. They did not know enough to separate, but kept close together, sometimes crowding and striking against each other in their furious efforts to escape.

But, after the chase had continued some time, one of the animals began to fall in the rear, and Johnny directed his attention toward him, as he would be the most easy to secure.

This fellow was a huge bull that was slightly lame, which accounted for his tardiness of gait. Frightened as he was, it was not that blind terror which had seized the Indians when they discovered the steam man so close at their heels. The bull was one of those creatures that if closely pressed would turn and charge the monster. He was not one to continue a fruitless flight, no matter who or what was his pursuer.

The boy was not aware of this sturdy trait in the animal, nor did he dream of anything like resistance.

50

So he steadily drew toward him, until within twenty yards, when he let go of his controlling rod, and picked up the rifle beside him. A bullet from this, he supposed, would kill any animal, however large, no matter at what portion of his body he aimed.

So raising partly to his feet, and steadying himself as well as he could, he aimed for the lumping haunch of the animal. The ball buried itself in his flank, and so retarded his speed, that the next moment the boy found himself beside him.

The instant this took place, the bull lowered his head, and without further warning, charged full at the steam man.

The boy saw the danger, but too late to stave it off. His immense head struck the rear of the monster with such momentum that he was lifted fully a foot from the ground, the concussion sounding like the crack of a pistol.

Fortunately the shock did not materially injure the machine, although the frightened boy expected to be capsized and killed by the infuriated buffalo.

The latter, when he had made his plunge, instantly drew back for another, which was sure to be fatal if made as fairly as the first. The boy retained his presence of mind enough to let on full steam, and the concern shot away at an extraordinary rate, bounding over the ground so furiously that the billets of wood were thrown and scattered in every direction, so that now, from being the pursuer, he had speedily become the pursued. The tables were turned with a vengeance!

It was only by providential good fortune that young Brainerd escaped instant destruction. The wonder was that the steam man was not so injured as to be unable to travel, in which case the maddened bull would have left little of him.

As it was, the experience of the boy was such as he could never forget. When he turned his affrighted glance behind he saw the enraged animal plunging furiously after him, his head lowered, his tongue out, his eyes glaring, and his whole appearance that of the most brutal ferocity.

Had the bull come in collision with the horse or man while in that mood he would have made short work of him.

But great as was his speed, it could not equal that of the wonderful steam man, who took such tremendous strides that a few minutes sufficed to carry him beyond all danger.

Johnny quietly slacked off steam, but he kept up a good swinging gait, not caring to renew his close acquaintance with his wounded enemy. The latter speedily discovered he was losing ground, and finally gave up the pursuit and trotted off at a leisurely rate to join his companions, apparently none the worse for the slight wound he had received.

As soon as the boy found himself beyond the reach of the animal's fury he halted the man and made a minute examination of the machinery.

The head and horns of the buffalo had dented the iron skin of the steam man, but the blow being distributed over a large area, inflicted no other damage, if indeed this could be called damage of itself.

The boy was greatly pleased, not only at his escape but at the admirable manner in which his invention had borne the shock of collision. It gave him a confidence in it which hitherto he had not felt.

Turning his face more toward the mountains, he again let on a good head of steam and rattled over the prairie at a stirring rate. An hour was sufficient to bring him to the base, where he halted.

He had not forgotten the warning of the trapper, but, like almost any inexperienced person, he could not see any cause for alarm. He scanned every part of the prairie and mountain that was in his field of vision, but could detect nothing alarming.

He supposed the parting admonition of Baldy was merely a general warning, such as a cautious person gives to one whom he has reason to fear is somewhat careless in his conduct.

It therefore required little self-argument upon his part after putting his man in proper "condition," to start off on a ramble up the mountain side. It was not his intention to remain more than an hour or so, unless he came across some game. He had a goodly quantity of ammunition, and was careful that his rifle was loaded, so as not to be taken unawares by any emergency.

Although Johnny Brainerd was afflicted with misshapen form, yet he was very quick and active upon his feet, and bounded along over the rocks, and across the chasms like a deer, with such a buoyancy of spirits that he forgot danger.

However, he had gone but a short distance, when he was

startled by a low fierce growl, and turning his head, saw to his horror, that he had nearly run against a colossal animal, which he at once recognized as the dreaded grizzly bear.

Such a meeting would have startled an experienced hunter, and it was therefore with no steady nerve that he hastily brought his piece to his shoulder and fired.

The shot struck the bear in the body, doing just what his shot at the buffalo had done some time before. It thoroughly angered him, without inflicting anything like a serious wound. With a growl of fury the brute made straight for him.

What would the boy have given, as he sped down the mountain side, were he now in his wagon, whirled over the prairie at a rate which would enable him to laugh to scorn any such speed as that of the brute.

At first he had hopes of reaching his refuge, but he was not long in seeing that it was impossible, and found that if he escaped he must find some refuge very speedily.

When he suddenly found himself beneath a goodly-sized tree it looked like a providential indication to him, and throwing his gun to the ground, he ascended the tree in the shortest time that he had ever made.

He was none too soon as it was, for the bear was so close beneath him that he felt the brush of its claws along his feet, as he nervously jerked them beyond its reach.

Hastily scrambling to the very top of the tree, he secured himself among the limbs, and then glanced down to see what his enemy was doing. Great was his relief to find him sitting on his haunches, contenting himself with merely casting wistful glances upward.

The sensation of even temporary safety was a relief, but when a full hour had dragged by, with scarcely a single change of position upon the part of the brute, Johnny began to ask himself what was to be the end of all this.

It looked as though the grizzly had resolved in making his dinner upon the youngster who had dared to fire a shot at him. The patience of an animal is proverbially greater than that of a human being, and that of the bear certainly exceeded to a great degree that of his expected prey who crouched in the limbs above.

# CHAPTER XII

# The Grizzly Bear

From where young Brainerd was perched on the tree it was impossible to catch a glimpse of the steam man, so patiently awaiting his return. The distance was also too great for him to make himself heard by the miners, who were hard at work twenty miles away.

Fruitful in expedients, it was not long before the boy found a resource in his trouble. Tearing a large strip from his coat, he tore this into smaller strips, until he had secured a rope half a dozen yards in length. Upon the end of this he placed a loop, and then, descending to the lowest limb, he devoted himself to the task of drooping it over the end of his gun. It fortunately had fallen in such a manner that the muzzle was somewhat elevated, so that here was a good opportunity for the exercise of his skill and patience.

When the first attempt was made the bear suddenly clawed at it and tore it from the boy's hand before he could jerk it beyond his reach. So he was compelled to make another one.

Nothing discouraged, the boy soon had this completed, and it was dropped down more cautiously than before. When the grizzly made a lunge at it, it was deftly twitched out of his way.

This was repeated several times, until the brute became disgusted with the sport, and dropping down behind the tree, let the boy do all the fishing he chose.

Now was his time, but the boy did not allow his eagerness to overcome the steadiness of his nerves. It required no little skill, but he finally succeeded in dropping the noose over the muzzle of the gun and jerked it up taut.

With a heart beating high with hope, Johnny saw it lifted clear of the ground, and he began carefully drawing it up. The grizzly looked curiously at his maneuvers, and once made as if to move toward the dangling rifle; but, ere his mind was settled, it was drawn beyond his reach, and the cold muzzle was grasped in the hand of the eagerly waiting boy.

While drawing it up, he had been debating with himself as to the best means of killing the brute. Remembering that his first shot had done no harm, he sensibly concluded that he had not yet learned the vulnerable part of the monster.

His gun was loaded very carefully, and when everything was ready he made a noise, to attract the attention of the brute. The bear looked up instantly, when the gun was aimed straight at his right eye.

Ere the grizzly could withdraw his gaze, the piece was discharged, and the bullet sped true, crashing into the skull of the colossal brute. With a howling grunt, he rose upon his hind feet, clawed the air a few moments, and then dropped dead.

Young Brainerd waited until he was certain that the last spark of life had fled, when he cautiously descended the tree, scarcely able to realize the truth that he had slain a grizzly bear, the monarch of the western wilderness. But such was the fact, and he felt more pride at the thought than if he had slain a dozen buffaloes.

"If I only had him in the wagon," he reflected, "I'd take him into camp, for they will never believe I killed a grizzly bear."

However, it occurred to him that he might secure some memento, and accordingly he cut several claws and placed them in his pocket. This done, he concluded that, as the afternoon was well advanced, it was time he started homeward.

His hurried flight from the ferocious brute had bewildered him somewhat, and, when he took the direction he judged to be the right one, he found nothing familiar or remembered, from which fact he concluded he was going astray.

But a little computation on his part, and he soon righted himself, and was walking along quite hopefully, when he received another severe shock of terror, at hearing the unmistakable whoop of an Indian, instantly followed by several others.

Immediately he recalled the warning given by the trapper, and looked furtively about, to make sure that he was not already in their hands. His great anxiety now was to reach the steam man and leave the neighborhood, which was rapidly becoming untenable.

So he began stealing forward as rapidly as possible, at the same time keeping a sharp lookout for danger. It required a half-hour, proceeding at this rate, before reaching the base of the mountain. The moment he did so, he looked all around in quest of the steam man, whom he had been compelled to desert for so long a time.

He discovered it standing several hundred yards away; but, to his dismay, there were fully a dozen Indians standing and walking about it, examining every portion with the greatest curiosity.

Here was a dilemma indeed, and the boy began to believe that he had gotten himself into an inextricable difficulty, for how to reach the steam man and renew the fire, under the circumstances, was a question which might well puzzle an older head to answer.

It was unfortunate that the machine should have been taken at this great disadvantage, for it was stripping it of its terror to those Indians, who were such inveterate enemies to the whites. They had probably viewed it with wonder and fear at first; but finding it undemonstrative, had gradually gathered courage, until they had congregated around it, and made as critical a scrutiny as they know how.

Whatever fear or terror they had felt at first sight was now gone; for they seemed on the most familiar terms with it.

Several climbed into the wagon, others passed in and around the helpless giant, and one valiant fellow hit him a thwack on the stomach with his tomahawk.

This blow hurt the boy far more than it did the iron man, and he could hardly repress a cry of pain, as he looked upon the destruction of his wonderful friend as almost inevitable.

The savage, however, contented himself with this demonstration, and immediately after walked away toward the mountain. The observant boy knew what this meant, and he withdrew from his temporary hiding-place, and started to watch him.

The fact that the Indian followed precisely the path taken by him, did not remove the uneasiness, and he made up his mind

that nothing but danger was to come to him from this proceeding.

When the Indian had reached the spot where the dead grizzly
bear lay, he paused in the greatest wonderment. Here was something which he did not understand.

The dead carcass showed that somebody had slain him, and
the shot in the eye looked as though it had been done by an
experienced hunter. A few minutes' examination of the ground
showed further that he who had fired the shot was in the tree at
the time, after which he had descended and fled.

All this took but a few minutes for the savage to discover,
when he gave a whoop of triumph at his success in probing the
matter, and started off on the trail.

Unluckily, this led straight toward the boulder behind which
the boy had concealed himself; and ere he could find a new
hiding-place the Indian was upon him.

At sight of the boy, the savage gave a whoop, and raised his
tomahawk; but the youngster was expecting this, and instantly
raising his gun, he discharged it full into his heart.

As he heard the shriek of the Indian, and saw him throw up
his arms, he did not wait to hear or see anything else, but
instantly fled with might and main, scarcely looking or knowing
whither he was going.

A short time after he found himself at the base of the mountain, very near the spot where he had first come, and glancing
again toward the steam man, he saw him standing motionless, as
before, and with not a single Indian in sight!

# CHAPTER XIII

## An Appalling Danger

Not a second was to be lost. The next moment the boy had run across the intervening space and pulled open the furnace door of the steam man. He saw a few embers yet smoldering in the bottom, enough to rekindle the wood. Dashing in a lot from the wagon, he saw it begin blazing up. He pulled the valve wide open, so that there might not be a moment's delay in starting, and held the water in the boiler at a proper level. The smoke immediately began issuing from the pipe or hat, and the hopes of the boy rose correspondingly.

The great danger was that the Indians would return before he could start. He kept glancing behind him, and it was with a heart beating with despair that he heard several whoops, and saw at the same instant a number of red-skins coming toward him.

The boy gave a jolt to the wagon, which communicated to the steam man, and it instantly started, at quite a moderate gait, but rapidly increased to its old-fashioned run.

It was just in the nick of time, for two minutes later the savages would have been upon him. As it was, when they saw the giant moving off they paused for a moment in amazement.

But their previous acquaintance with the apparatus had robbed it of all its supernatural attributes, and their halt lasted but a few seconds. The next moment they understood that there was some human agency about it, and uttering their blood-curdling yells, they started in full pursuit. But by this time the steam gentleman was getting down to his regular pace, and was striding over the prairie like a dromedary. For a time the Indians gained, then the intervening distance became stationary, and then he began pulling steadily away from them.

Still the savages maintained the chase until satisfied of its hopelessness, when they gave it up and sullenly withdrew in the direction of the mountains.

The young fellow, in his triumph, could not avoid rising in the wagon, shouting and waving his hat defiantly at his baffled pursuers. The daring act came near costing his life, for it was instantly followed by the discharge of several guns, and the singing of the bullets about his ears caused him to duck back into his seat as suddenly as he had risen from it.

The afternoon was now quite well advanced, and besides feeling hungry, Johnny Brainerd was anxious to get back to camp.

The intervening distance was rapidly passed, and the sun was just setting as he slacked up within a short distance of Wolf Ravine.

For some unaccountable reason, the nearer he approached "camp," as it was called, a feeling akin to fear came over him. It was a presentiment of coming evil, which he found it impossible either to shake off or to define, and that was why he halted some distance away.

From where he stood it was impossible to see his two friends at work, but at that time of day he knew they were accustomed to stop work and come out upon the prairie for the purpose of enjoying the cool breeze of evening. At the same time, when such constant danger threatened, they were accustomed to have one of their number, either all or a part of the time, on the ground above, where the approach of enemies could be detected.

The absence of anything like a sentinel increased the boy's apprehensions, and when he had waited some fifteen minutes without seeing anything of his friends he became painfully uneasy.

"What if they had been killed? What if they were prisoners? What if a hundred Indians were at that moment in the possession of Wolf Ravine?

Such and similar were the questions which the affrighted boy asked himself, and which, with all his shrewdness, he was unable to answer.

In the hope of attracting attention he set up a shrieking with the whistle, which sounded so loud on the still evening air that it must have gone miles away over the level prairie.

There being no response to this he kept it up for some time, but it still failed, and all this confirmed him in the belief that "something was up."

What that particular something was it was impossible to say, so long as he sat in the wagon, and for five minutes he endeavored to decide whether it was best to get out and make a reconnaissance on his own hook or remain where, in case of danger, he could seek safety in flight.

As the day wore rapidly away, and he still failed to see or hear anything of his friends, he finally concluded to get out and make an examination of the ravine.

Accordingly he sprung lightly to the ground, but had scarcely alighted when a peculiar signal, something resembling a tremulous whistle, reached his ear, and he instantly clambered back again, fully satisfied that the whistle was intended as a signal, and that it concerned him, although whether from friend or foe he could only conjecture.

However, his alarm was such that he moved a hundred yards or so further away from the ravine, where there was less likelihood of being surprised by any sudden rush upon the part of the thieving red-skins.

From this standpoint he carefully scanned what could be seen of the ravine. It descended quite gradually from the edge of the bank, so that he gained a partial view of the rocks and boulders upon the opposite side. Some of the trees growing in the narrow valley rose to such a height that one-half or two-thirds of them were exposed to view.

It was while the boy was gazing at these that he detected a peculiar movement in one of the limbs, which instantly arrested his attention.

A moment showed him that the peculiar waving motion was made by human agency, and he strained his eyes in the hope of detecting the cause of the curious movement.

The gathering darkness made his vision quite uncertain; but he either saw, or fancied he saw, a dark object among the limbs which resembled the form of Baldy Bicknell, the trapper.

Johnny Brainerd would have given almost anything in the world could he have understood what it all meant.

But the very fact of these singular demonstrations was prima facie evidence of the most unquestionable kind; and, after a moment's consultation with himself, he began moving away, just as the sharp crack of several rifles notified him of the fearful peril which he had escaped.

# CHAPTER XIV

# The Huge Hunter

Simultaneous with the report of the rifles came the pinging of the bullets about the ears of young Brainerd, who, having started the steam man, kept on going until he was a considerable distance from the ravine.

All the time he kept looking back, but could see nothing of his enemies, nor could he detect the point from which the rifle-shots were fired.

Now, as night descended over the prairie, and the retreat of his friends became shrouded in impenetrable darkness, he fully appreciated the fact that not only were they in great danger, but so was he himself.

The heathenish terror with which the steam man had at first inspired the savages had rapidly worn away, the circumstances unfortunately having been such that they had very speedily learned that it was nothing more than a human invention, which of itself could accomplish little or no harm.

He could but reflect, as the man glided slowly along, that if he had the three friends beside him, how easily they could glide away in the darkness and leave all danger behind.

But they were in the extremity of peril already, and, reflect and cogitate as much as he chose, he could see no earthly way of assisting them out of their difficulty.

Besides the concern which he naturally felt regarding his friends, there was a matter that more clearly related to himself that demanded his attention.

The water in the tank was at its lowest ebb, and it would be dangerous for him to attempt to run more than one hour or so longer before replenishing it. Consequently he was unable to stand anything like another chase from the Indians.

As the part of prudence, therefore, he turned toward the river, following slowly along the bank, in quest of some place where it would be easy and safe for him to secure the much-needed water.

It was a long and discouraging hunt. The banks were so high that he could find no point where it was safe for him to descend to the water's edge. There was too great a risk of "upsetting his cart," a calamity which, in all probability, would be irreparable.

At length, however, when he had wandered about a mile distant from the Wolf Ravine, he discovered a place, where the bank had about six feet elevation, and sloped down gradually to the river.

Here he paused, and with a small vessel, descended to the stream, muttering to himself as he did so:

"Why didn't I think and put a pumping arrangement to the machine? I could have done it as well as not, and it would have saved me a good deal of trouble."

But regrets were now unavailing, and he lost no time in useless lamentations, setting to work at once. It was tedious labor, carrying up the water in a small vessel, and emptying it in the tank, but he persevered, and at the end of a couple of hours the task was completed.

"I can make the wood stand me another day," he added, as he stood looking at the greatly diminished pile, "although, if I knew where to get it, I would load up now, and then I should be prepared."

He suddenly paused, for scarcely a dozen yards away, coming up the margin of the river, straight toward him, he descried the figure of a man fully six feet and a half high.

Young Brainerd's first impulse was to spring into the wagon and start away at full speed; but a second glance showed him that it was not an Indian, but a white man, in the garb of a hunter.

"Hullo, boss, thar, what yer doin'?"

He was at a loss what reply to make, and therefore made none. The next moment the giant hunter was beside him.

"B'ars and bufflers! younker, what ye got thar?" he demanded, eyeing the steam man with an expression of the most amazed wonder. "I say, what do yer call that thing?"

"That," laughed Johnny, who could not avoid a feeling of strong apprehension at the singular appearance of the strange hunter, "is a sort of peregrinating locomotive."

"Paggyratin' locomotive, what's that?" he asked, in a gruff voice, and with an expression of great disgust at the unfamiliar words employed.

"You have seen a locomotive, haven't you?"

"Reckon I hev, down in St. Louey."

"Well, this is something on the same principle, except that it uses legs instead of wheels."

"Can that ere thing walk?"

"Yes, sir, and run, too; it traveled all the way from the Missouri river to this place."

The huge hunter turned upon him with a fierce expression.

"Yer can't fool this yar boss in that style."

"Don't you believe me?" asked the boy, who was fearful of offending the stranger.

"No, sar; not a word."

"How do you suppose we got it here?"

"Fotched in a wagon."

"Let me show you what he can do."

He was about to step into the wagon, when the hunter stopped him.

"See hyar, younker, who mought yer be?"

The boy gave his name and residence.

"What yer doin' hyar?"

"I'm traveling with this machine of mine."

"How do you git it along?"

"I was just going to show you when you stopped me."

"Hold on; no need of bein' in a sweat about it. Do yer come alone?"

"No. I came with a hunter."

"What war his name?"

"Baldy Bicknell."

"B'ars and bufflers! did yer come with him?"

"Yes; he was my companion all the way."

"Whar mought he be?"

Johnny Brainerd hesitated a moment. While the huge hunter might possibly be of great service to the beleaguered miners, yet he recollected that it was the desire of Baldy that the fact of gold existing in Wolf Ravine should be kept a secret from all except their own party.

Should it become known to any of the numerous hunters and emigrants who were constantly passing in the neighborhood, there would be such a flocking to the place that they would be driven away and probably killed for the treasure that they had already obtained.

The boy, therefore, chose to make a non-committal reply:

"Baldy is some distance away, in camp."

"And what are yer doin' hyar?"

"I stopped here to get water for this steam man, as we call him. You know anything that travels by steam must have the water to generate it."

"I say, younker, I don't want none of yer big words to me. Ef I h'ar any more, b'ars and bufflers, ef I don't crack yer over the head with Sweetlove, my shootin'-iron, so mind what yer say, fur I won't stand no nonsense."

"I didn't wish to offend you," returned the boy, in the meekest of tones.

"How far away might be Baldy?"

"I couldn't tell you exactly, but I think it is less than ten miles."

"Be you goin' back to camp to-night?"

"It was my intention, that is, I meant to do so."

"Guess I'll go with yer; but see hyar, younker, let's see yer try that old humbug of yourn."

The boy sprung into the wagon, glad of the opportunity of getting rid of what looked like a dangerous man. Before he could start he was again peremptorily stopped.

"Yer see, I b'leeve yar a humbug, but if that ole thing does run, and, mind, I tell yer, I don't b'leeve it will, do yer know what I'm goin' to do?"

"I do not."

"I'm goin' to take it myself to chase rod-skins in. It won't bother yer much fur them long legs of yourn to carry that humpback home again. So, younker, start now, and let us see what yer can do."

The boy let on steam, and the man started off on a moderate gait, which rapidly increased to a swift one. The huge, wonder-stricken hunter watched it until it gradually faded out of sight in the gloom, and still watched the place where it had disappeared, and though he watched much longer, with a savage and vindictive heart, yet it never came back to him again.

# CHAPTER XV

# The Attack in the Ravine

In the mean time, the situation of our friends in Wolf Ravine was becoming perilous to the last degree.

Before going to work, on the morning of the steam man's excursion to the mountains, Baldy Bicknell made a reconnaissance of the ravine, to assure himself that there was no danger of being suddenly overwhelmed, while delving for the precious yellow sand.

He saw abundant signs of Indians having recently visited the place, but he concluded there were none in the immediate vicinity, and that comparatively little risk was run in the boy making his wished-for visit to the mountains in the west.

Through the center of the ravine ran a small stream of water, hardly of enough volume to be used for washing gold without a dam being created. It looked as if this had once been the head of a large stream, and that the golden sand had been drifted to this spot, by the force of the powerful current.

The auriferous particles were scattered over the entire breadth of the ravine, for the distance of several hundred feet, being found in the richest deposits between the ledges and rocks, in the bottom of the channel, where, as may well be supposed, it was no easy matter to obtain.

A short distance back of the "diggings," where the vast masses of rocks assumed curiously grotesque forms, the miners discovered a rude cave, where they at once established their headquarters. A tiny stream ran through the bottom of it, and with a little placing of the close boulders, they speedily put it in the best condition of defense.

It was almost entirely surrounded by trees, there was one spot where a thin man, like Hopkins or Baldy, could draw his body through and climb a luxuriant cottonwood, whose top had a wide view of the surrounding plain.

The day passed away without any signs of Indians, Baldy occasionally ascending the side of the ravine, and scanning the plains in every direction, on the constant lookout for the insidious approach of their enemies.

Just before nightfall, while all three were at work, a rifle was discharged, and the bullet was imbedded in the tough oaken handle of the spade with which the trapper was digging.

"Whar in thunder did that come from?" he demanded, dropping the implement, catching up the rifle, and glaring savagely about him.

But neither of the others could answer him, and climbing up the bank, he looked fiercely around for some evidence of the whereabouts of his treacherous foe.

The latter remained invisible, but several hundred yards down the ravine, he caught a glimpse of enough Indians dodging hither and thither to satisfy him that there was quite a formidable force in the valley.

Giving the alarm to his companions, all three withdrew within the cave, not the less willingly, as it was very near their usual quitting time.

"Begorrah! and what'll becoom of the shtame mian and the boy?" inquired Mickey, as he hastily obeyed orders.

"Jerusalem!" exclaimed the Yankee, in great trepidation, "if he isn't warned, they'll catch him sure, and then what'll become of us? We'll have to walk all the way hum."

As the best means of communicating with him, the trapper climbed through the narrow opening, and to the top of the tree, where he ensconced himself, just as the steam man uttered its interrogative whistle.

The trapper, as we have shown in another place, replied by pantomime, not wishing to discover his whereabouts to the enemy, as he had a dim idea that this means of egress might possibly prove of some use to him, in the danger that was closing around them.

When Johnny Brainerd recognized his signal, and beat a

retreat, Baldy began a cautious descent to his cave again. At this time it was already growing dark, and he had to feel his way down again.

And so it came about, that not until he had reached the lowest limb, did his trained ear detect a slight rustling on the ground beneath. Supposing it to be either Mickey or Ethan, he continued his descent, merely glancing below. But at that moment something suspicious caught his eye, and peering down more carefully, he discovered a crouching Indian, waiting with drawn knife until he should come within his reach.

The trapper was no coward, and had been in many a hand to-hand tussle before; but there was something in the character of the danger which would have made it more pleasant for him to hesitate awhile until he could learn its precise dimensions; but time was too precious, and the next moment, he had dropped directly by the side of the red-skin.

The latter intended to make the attack, but without waiting for him, Baldy sprung like a panther upon him and bore him to the earth. There was a silent but terrific struggle for a few moments, but the prodigious activity and rower of the trapper prevailed, and when he withdrew from the grasp of the Indian, the latter was as dead as a door nail. The struggle had been so short that neither Mickey nor Ethan knew anything of it, until Baldy dropped down among them, and announced what had taken place.

"Jerusalem! have they come as close as that?" asked the Yankee in considerable terror.

"Skulp me, if they ain't all around us!" was the reply of the hunter.

"How we ar' to git out o' hyar, ar' a hard thing to tell j'ist now."

"It's meself that thinks the rid gentlemin have a love fur us, as me mither obsarved, when she cracked the head of me father," remarked Mickey, who had seated himself upon the ground with all the indifference of an unconcerned spectator.

It was so dark in their cave-like home that they could not see each other's faces, and could only catch a sort of twilight glimpse of their forms when they passed close to each other.

It would have made their quarters more pleasant had they struck a light, but it was too dangerous a proceeding, and no one thought of it. They could only keep on the alert, and watch for the movement of their enemies.

The latter, beyond all doubt, were in the immediate vicinity, and inspired as they were by hate of the most vindictive kind, would not allow an opportunity to pass of doing all the harm in their power.

The remains of their food was silently eaten in the darkness, when Baldy said:

"Do yer stay hyar whar ye be till I come back."

"Where might ye be going naow?" inquired Hopkins.

"I'm goin' outside to see what the reds are doin', and to see whether thar's a chance fur 'em to gobble us up hull."

"Do yees mind and take care of y'urself, as me mither cautioned me when I went a shparkin'," said Mickey, who naturally felt some apprehension, when he saw the trapper on the point of leaving them at such a dangerous time.

"Yes. Baldy, remember that my fate is wrapped up in yours," added the Yankee, whose sympathies were probably excited to a still greater extent.

"Never mind about Baldy; he has been in such business too often not to know how to take care of himself."

"How long do you expect to be gone?" inquired Ethan.

"Mebbe all night, if thar ain't much danger. Ef I find the varments ar' too thick I'll stay by yer, and if they ain't I'll leave fur several hours. Leastways, whatever I do, you'll be sure to look out for the skunks."

With this parting admonition, the trapper withdrew.

In going out, he made his exit by the same entrance by which all had come in. He proceeded with great caution, for none knew better than he the danger of a single misstep. He succeeded, after considerable time, in reaching a portion of the valley so shrouded in gloom that he was able to advance without fear of discovery.

He thoroughly reconnoitered every part of the ravine in the immediate vicinity of the cave, but could discover nothing of the Indians, and he concluded that they were some distance away.

Having assured himself of this, the trapper cautiously ascended the side of the ravine, until he reached the open prairie, when he lost no time in leaving the dangerous place behind him.

He had no intention, however, of deserting his friends, but had simply gone in quest of the steam man. He comprehended the difficulty under which they all labored, so long as they were annoyed in this manner by the constant attacks of the savages, and he had an idea that the invention of the dwarfed Johnny Brainerd could be turned to a good account in driving the miscreants away so thoroughly that they would remain away for a long enough time for them to accomplish something in the way of gathering the wealth lying all about them.

He recalled the direction which he had seen the puffing giant take, and he bent his steps accordingly, with only a faint hope of meeting him without searching the entire night for him. Baldy was shrewd enough to reason that as the boy would wish some water for his engine, he would remain in the immediate vicinity of the river until at least that want could be supplied.

Acting on this supposition, he made his way to the river bank, and followed so closely to the water that its moonlit surface was constantly visible to him.

The night was still, and, as he moved silently along, he often paused and listened, hoping to hear the familiar rattle of the wheels, as the youngster sped over the prairie.

Without either party knowing it, he passed within a few yards of Duff McIntosh, the huge trapper, whom he had known so intimately years before.

But had he been aware of the fact, he would only have turned further aside, to avoid him; for, when the two trappers, several years previous, separated, they had been engaged in a deadly quarrel, which came near resulting fatally to both.

At length the faint rattle of the wheels caught his ear, and he bent his steps toward the point where he judged the steam man to be.

# CHAPTER XVI

# The Repulse

A few minutes more satisfied the trapper that he was right. Gradually out from the darkness the approaching figure resolved itself into the steam man.

Johnny Brainerd, after leaving the huge trapper so neatly, continued wandering aimlessly over the prairie at a moderate speed, so as to guard against the insidious approach of the Indians, or the hunter who had threatened to confiscate his property in so unjustifiable a manner.

Fortunately he did not see Baldy until the latter cautiously hailed him, otherwise he would have fled before ascertaining his identity; but the moment he recognized his voice he hastened toward him, no less surprised than pleased at meeting him so unexpectedly.

"Where are Mickey and Ethan?" he inquired, as he leaped alongside of him.

"In the cave."

"How is it you are here?"

The trapper briefly explained that he had crept out to hunt him up; but as there seemed no imminent danger, he deemed it best to leave his companions there, as if the Indians once gained possession of the golden ravine, it would be difficult, if not impossible, to displace them.

Besides, in order to carry out the scheme which he had formed, it was necessary that two at least should remain in the cave, while the others were on the outside.

Under the direction of the trapper, the steam man slowly approached the ravine, keeping at a respectful distance, but so near that if any sudden emergency should arise, they would be able to render assistance to their friends.

The boy gave several whistles so as to inform the Irishman and Yankee of their whereabouts. A few seconds after, and while the noise of the instrument was echoing over the prairie, a fainter whistle reached their ears.

"That's the long-legged Yankee!" instantly remarked the trapper; "he knows how to make my kind of noise."

"What does it mean?"

"It means that all is right."

"Where are the Indians?"

"They ain't fur off. I wish they war further, fur ef it warn't fur them, we'd had half the yaller metal out of thar by this time."

Young Brainerd had the reputation of possessing a remarkably keen vision; but, peer as much as he might, he could detect nothing unusual. The trapper, however, affirmed that numerous forms could be seen creeping along the edge of the prairie, and that these same forms were more nor less than so many red-skins.

"What are they trying to do?"

"Duono."

"Hadn't we better withdraw?" inquired Johnny, showing a little nervousness.

"Not till we know they're after us," was the quiet reply.

By and by the boy himself was able to get an occasional glimpse of the shadowy figures moving to and fro.

"I think they are going to surround us," he added, "and I feel as though we ought to get out while we can do so."

The only reply to this, was by the trapper suddenly bringing his gun to his shoulder and firing. An agonizing screech, as the savage threw himself in the air, showed that the shot had not been in vain.

Rather curiously at the same moment the report of a gun in the ravine reached their ears, followed by the same death-shriek.

"They ain't sleepin' very powerful down thar," was the pleased remark of the trapper, as he leisurely reloaded his piece, while the boy remained in that nervous state, awaiting the permission of Baldy to go spinning away over the prairie at a rate that would very quickly carry him beyond all danger.

But the trapper was in no hurry to give the ardently desired permission. He seemed to have a lingering affection for the place, which prevented his "tearing himself away."

The boy's timidity was not in the least diminished, when several return shots were fired, the bullets pinging all around them.

"My gracious, Baldy, let's get out of this!" he instantly pleaded, starting the man himself.

"Go about fifty feet," was the reply, "but not any further."

It may be said that the steam man fairly leaped over this space, and somewhat further, like a frightened kangaroo, and even then it would not have halted had not the trapper given peremptory orders for it to do so.

The sky was now clear and the moon, riding high and nearly full, illumined the prairie for a considerable distance, and there was no fear but that they could detect the approach of the most treacherous savage, let him come in whatever disguise he chose.

The night wore gradually away, without any particular demonstration upon the part of either the Indians or white men, although dropping shots were occasionally exchanged, without any particular result on either side.

Now and then a red-skin, creeping cautiously along, made his appearance on the edge of the ravine; but there was too much light for him to expose himself to the deadly rifle of the trapper, who took a kind of savage pleasure in sending his leaden messengers after the aborigines.

This species of sport was not without its attendant excitement and danger; for the last creature to take a shot quietly is an American Indian; and they kept popping away at the steam man and its train whenever a good opportunity offered.

Owing to the size and peculiar appearance of the steamer, he was a fair target for his enemies; and, indeed, so uncomfortably close did some of the bullets come, that the boy almost continually kept his head lowered, so as to be protected by the sides of the wagon.

Finally morning came, greatly to the relief of all our friends. As soon as it was fairly light the Irishman and Yankee were notified that a move was about to be made, by means of the steam-whistle. An answering signal coming back to them, the steam man at once advanced to the very edge of the ravine.

The trapper peering cautiously down the gulch, caught sight of several red-skins crouching near the cave, and, directing young Brainerd to discharge his piece at a certain one, the two fired nearly together. Scarce five seconds had elapsed, when both Ethan and Mickey did the same. All four, or rather three, as the boy gave his principal attention to the engine, began loading and firing as rapidly as possible.

The red-skins returned a few scattering shots; but they were taken at such disadvantage, that they immediately began a precipitate retreat down the ravine.

Ere they had withdrawn a hundred yards, Ethan and Mickey emerged from the cave, shouting and excited, firing at every red-skin they could see, the Irishman occasionally swinging his gun over his head, and daring the savages to a hand-to-hand encounter.

While the two were thus engaged, the trapper was not idle. The steam man maintained his place but a short distance behind the enemies, and his deadly rifle scarcely ever failed of its mark.

The moment an Indian was killed or helplessly wounded, his companions caught and dragged him away, there being a great fear upon the part of all that some of their number might fall into the hands of their enemies, and suffer the ineffaceable disgrace of being scalped.

The savages were followed a long distance, until their number had diminished down to a fraction of what it was originally, and the survivors had all they could do in taking care of their disabled comrades.

Never was victory more complete. The Indians were thoroughly discomfited, and only too glad to get away after being so severely punished. During this singular running fight the steam man kept up a constant shrieking, which doubtless contributed in no slight degree to the rout of the red-skins. They fired continually at the fearful-looking monster, and, finding their shots produced no effect, invested the thing with a portion of the supernatural power which they had given it at first sight.

When the last glimpse of the retreating Indians was seen, the trapper turned triumphantly toward the boy.

"Warn't that purty well done, younker?"

"It was indeed."

"They'll now stay away awhile."

"We would have failed if we had waited any longer."

"Why so, boy?"

"Because the last stick is burned, and the steam man couldn't be made to run a mile further without more fuel."

# CHAPTER XVII

## Homeward Bound

The punishment administered to the Indians who had so greatly annoyed the miners proved a very beneficial one.

Nothing more was seen of them, except one or two glimpses of the red-skin upon his black horse. He, however, maintained a respectful distance, and at the end of a day or two disappeared altogether.

These were golden moments indeed to the miners, and they improved them to the utmost. From earliest light until the darkness of night they toiled almost unceasingly. Half the time they went hungry rather than stop their work to procure that which was so much needed. When, however, the wants of nature could no longer be trifled with, Baldy took his rifle and started off on a hunt, which was sure to be brief and successful.

Sometimes he caught sight of some game in the gulch, and sometimes something in the air drew the fire of his unerring rifle, and the miners feasted and worked as only such violently laboring men can do.

Although the boy was unable to assist at the severe labor, yet he soon demonstrated his genius and usefulness. He not only constructed a dam, but made a "rocker," or machine, of an original style, that did the work far more expeditiously and thoroughly than it had yet been done.

While the men were getting the auriferous sand, he separated it from the particles of dirt and gravel, without any assistance from them, and without any severe labor for himself.

There was some apprehension upon the part of all that the huge trapper, whom young Brainerd had met at night, would make his appearance. Should he do so, it would be certain to precipitate a difficulty of the worst kind, as he was morose, sullen, treacherous, envious and reckless of danger.

Baldy Bicknell really feared him more than he did the Indians, and the constant watchfulness he exercised for several days showed how great was his apprehension.

Fortunately, indeed, for all concerned, the giant hunter continued his travels in a different direction, and the miners were undisturbed by him.

Two weeks passed, by the end of which time the ravine was about exhausted of its precious stuff, and the miners made their preparations for going home.

It was impossible to do anything more than conjecture the amount of wealth they had obtained, but Baldy was sure that there was enough, when sold, to buy each of them a handsome farm.

"Jerusalem! but naow ain't that good?" exclaimed the delighted Ethan Hopkins, as he mopped off his perspiring forehead. "That 'ere encourages me to take a step that I've often contemplated."

"What might the same be?"

"Git married: me and Seraphenia Pike hev been engaged for the last ten years, and now I'll be hanged ef I don't go home and get spliced."

"And it's myself that'll do the same," added Mickey, as he executed an Irish jig on the barren earth in front of their cavern home, after they had concluded to leave the place.

"Where does she reside?" inquired Ethan.

"Ballyduff, Kings County, in the Oim of the Sea; it's there that lives the lass that's to have the honor of becoming Mrs. McSquizzle, and becomin' the mither of her own children. Arrah, but isn't the same a beauty?"

"The same as my own, Michael," ventured the Yankee, who deemed it his duty to correct this general remark of his friend.

"Arrah, now, get cut wid ye! she can't begin wid Miss Bridget Moghlaghigbogh that resides wid her mither and two pigs on the outskirts of Ballyduff, in the wee cabin that has the one room and the one windy. Warrah, warrah, now isn't she a jewel?"

"And so is Seraphenia."

"But has she the rid hair, that makes it onnecessary for them to have the candle lit at night? and has she the same beautiful freckles, the size of a ha'penny, on the face and the nose, that has such an iligant turn up at the end, that she used to hang her bonnet on it? Arrah, now, and didn't she have the swate teeth, six of the same that were so broad that they filled her mouth, and it was none of yer gimblet holes that was her mouth, but a beautiful one, that, when she smiled went round to her ears, did the same. And her shoes! but you orter seen them."

"Why so?"

"What was the matter with her shoes?"

"Nothing was the same. They was the shoes that the little pigs went to slaap in, afore they got so big that they couldn't git in them, and then it was her brother that used one of them same for a trunk when he emigrated to Amenity. Arrah, now, but wasn't me own Bridget a jewel?"

"Jehosephat! I should think she was!" exclaimed Hopkins, who had listened in amazement to this enumeration of the beauties of the gentle Irish lass, who had won the affections of Mickey McSquizzle. "No doubt she had a sweet disposition."

"Indeed she had, had she; it was that of an angel, was the same. It was niver that I staid there a night coorting the same that she didn't smash her shillaleh to smithereens over me head. Do yees observe that?" asked Mickey, removing his hat, and displaying a scar that extended half way across his head.

"I don't see how anyone can help seeing that."

"Well, that was the parting salute of Bridget, as I started for Ameriky. Arrah, now, but she did the same in style."

"That was her parting memento, was it?"

"Yes; I gave her the black eye, and she did the same fur me, and I niver takes off me hat to scratch me head that I don't think of the swate gal that I left at home."

And thereupon the Irishman began whistling "The Girl I Left Behind Me," accompanying it with a sort of waltzing dance, kept with remarkably good time.

"And so you intend to marry her?" inquired Hopkins, with no little amazement.

"It's that I do, ef I finds her heart fraa when I return to Ballyduff. You know, that the loikes of her is sought by all the lads in Kings County, and to save braaking their hearts, she may share the shanty of some of 'em."

"Jerusalem! but she is the all-firedest critter I ever heard tell on."

"What does ye maan by that?" demanded the Irishman, instantly flaring up; "does ye maan to insinooate that she isn't the most charming craater in the whole counthry?"

"You'll allow me to except my own Seraphenia?"

"Niver a once."

"Then I'll do it whether you like it or not. Your gal can't begin with mine, and never could."

"That I don't allow any man to say."

And the Irishman immediately began divesting himself of his coat, preparatory to settling the difference in the characteristic Irish manner. Nothing loth, the Yankee put himself in attitude, determined to stand up for the rights of his fair one, no matter by whom assailed.

Matters having progressed so far, there undoubtedly would have been a set-to between them, had not the trapper interfered. He and the boy were engaged in preparing the steam man and wagon for starting, when the excited words drew their attention, and seeing that a fight was imminent, Baldy advanced to where they stood and said:

"Not another word, or skulpme ef I don't hammer both of you till thar's nothin left o' you."

This was unequivocal language, and neither of the combatants misunderstood it. All belligerent manifestations ceased at once, and they turned to in assisting in the preparations for moving.

When all four were seated in the wagon, with their necessary baggage about them, it was found that there was comparatively little room for the wood. When they had stored all that they could well carry, it was found that there was hardly enough to last them twelve hours, so that there was considerable risk run from this single fact.

The steam man, however, stepped off with as much ease as when drawing the wagon with a single occupant. The boy let on enough of steam to keep up a rattling pace, and to give the assurance that they were progressing homeward in the fastest manner possible.

Toward the middle of the afternoon a storm suddenly came up and the rain poured in torrents.

As the best they could do, they took refuge in a grove, where, by stretching the canvas over themselves and the steam man, they managed to keep free from the wet.

The steam man was not intended to travel during stormy weather, and so they allowed him to rest.

# CHAPTER XVIII

# The Encampment

The storm proved the severest which the steam man had encountered since leaving St. Louis, and it put an effectual veto on his travels during its continuance, and for a short time afterward.

The prairie was found so soft and slippery that they were compelled to lie by until the sun had hardened it somewhat, when they once more resumed their journey.

As they now had thousands of dollars in their possession, and as all sorts of characters were found on the western plains, it may be said that none of the company ever felt easy.

Baldy Bicknell, the trapper, from his extensive experience and knowledge of the West, was the guide and authority on all matters regarding their travels. He generally kept watch during the night, obtaining what sleep he could through the day. The latter, however, was generally very precarious, as at sight of every horseman or cloud of smoke, they generally awakened him, so as to be sure and commit no serious error.

As the steam man would in all probability attract an attention that might prove exceedingly perilous to the gold in their possession, the trapper concluded it prudent to avoid the regular emigrant routes. Accordingly they turned well to the northward, it being their purpose to strike the Missouri, where they would be pretty sure of intercepting some steamer. Reaching such a place they would unjoint and take apart the steam man, packing it up in such a manner that no one could suspect its identity, and embark for St. Louis.

While this relieved them of the danger from their own race, it increased the probability of an attack upon the Indians, who scarcely ever seemed out of sight.

Their watchfulness, however, was constant, and it was due to this fact, more than any other, that they escaped attack at night for the greater part of their return journey.

Their position in the wagon was so cramped, that the party frequently became excessively wearied, and springing out, trotted and walked for miles alongside the tireless steam giant. Water was abundant, but several times they were put to great inconvenience to obtain wood. On three occasions they were compelled to halt for half a day in order to obtain the necessary supply.

Once the steam man came to a dead standstill in the open prairie, and narrowly escaped blowing up. A hasty examination upon the part of the inventor, revealed the fact that a leak had occurred in the tank, and every drop had run out.

This necessitated the greatest work of all, as water was carried the better part of a mile, and nearly an entire day consumed before enough steam could be raised to induce him to travel to the river, to procure it himself, while the miners acted as convoys.

Late one afternoon, they reached a singular formation in the prairie. It was so rough and uneven that they proceeded with great difficulty and at a slow rate of speed. While advancing in this manner, they found they had unconsciously entered a small narrow valley, the bottom of which was as level as a ground floor. The sides contracted until less than a hundred feet separated them, while they rose to the height of some eight or ten feet, and the bottom remained compact and firm, making it such easy traveling for the steam man, that the company followed down the valley, at a slow pace, each, however, feeling some misgiving as to the propriety of the course.

"It runs in the right direction," said young Brainerd, "and if it only keeps on as it began, it will prove a very handy thing for us."

"Hyar's as afeared it ain't goin' to keep on in that style," remarked Baldy; "howsumever, you can go ahead awhile longer."

"Naow, that's what I call real queer," remarked Ethan Hopkins, who was stretching his legs by walking alongside the steamer.

"And it's meself that thinks the same," added Mickey, puffing away at his short black pipe. "I don't understand it, as me father obsarved when they found fault with him for breaking another man's head."

"Ef we git into trouble, all we've got ta do is to back out," remarked Baldy, as a sort of apology for continuing his advance.

"This fellow doesn't know how to go backward," said Johnny, "but if it prove necessary, we can manage to turn him round."

"All right, go ahead."

At the same moment, the limber Yankee sprung into the wagon, and the steam man started ahead at a speed which was as fast as was prudent.

However, this delightful means of progress was brought to an unexpected standstill, by the sudden and abrupt termination of the valley. It ended completely as though it were an uncompleted canal, the valley rising so quickly to the level of the prairie, that there was no advancing any further, nor turning, nor in fact was there any possible way of extricating themselves from the difficulty, except by working the steam man around, and withdrawing by the same path that they had entered by.

"Well, here we are" remarked the boy, as they came to a standstill, "and what is to be done?"

"Get out of it," was the reply of Hopkins, who advanced several yards further, until he came up on the prairie again, so as to make sure of the exact contour of the ground.

"Did yer ever try to make the thing go up hill?" asked the trapper.

Young Brainerd shook his head. "Impossible! he would fall over on us, the minute it was attempted. When I was at work at first making him, what do you think was the hardest thing for me to do?"

"Make him go, I s'pose."

"That was difficult, but it was harder work to balance him, that is, so when he lifted up one foot he wouldn't immediately fall over on the same side. I got it fixed after a while, so that he ran as evenly and firmly as an engine, but I didn't fix upon any plan by which he could ascend or descend a hill."

"Can't you make him do it?"

"Not until he is made over again. I would be afraid to attempt to walk him up a moderate inclination, and know it would be sure destruction to start him up such a steep bank as that."

"Then we must work him round, I s'pose."

"There is nothing else that can be done."

"Let's at it, then."

This proved as difficult a job as they imagined. The steam man was so heavy that it was impossible to lift him, but he was shied around as much as possible; and, by the time he had walked across the valley he had half turned round.

He was then coaxed and worked back a short distance, when, with the "leverage" thus gained, the feat was completed, and the steam man stood with his face turned, ready to speed backward the moment that the word might be given.

By this time, however, the day was gone, and darkness was settling over the prairie. Quite a brisk breeze was blowing, and, as the position of the party was sheltered against this annoyance, Hopkins proposed that they should remain where they were until morning.

"We couldn't get a better place," said Johnny Brainerd, who was quite taken with the idea.

"It's a good place and it's a bad one," replied the trapper, who had not yet made up his mind upon the point.

They inquired what he meant by calling it a bad place.

"Ef a lot of the varmints should find we're hyar, don't you see what a purty fix they'd have us in?"

"It would be something like the same box in which we caught them in Wolf Ravine," said young Brainerd.

"Jist the same, perzactly."

"Not the same, either," said Hopkins; "we've got a better chance of getting out than they had. We can jump into the wagon and travel, while they can't; there's the difference."

"S'pose they git down thar ahead of us, how ar' we goin' to git away from them then?"

"Run over them."

"Don't know whether the younker has fixed the engine so it'll run over the skunks, ef it doesn't run up hill."

"It can be made to do that, I think," laughed young Brainerd.

"Afore we stay hyar, I'll take a look round to make sure that thar's some show for us."

The trapper ascended the bank, and, while his companions were occupied in their preparations for encamping, he examined the whole horizon and intervening space, so far as the human eye was capable of doing it. Finding nothing suspicious, he announced to his companions that they would remain where they were until morning.

# CHAPTER XIX

## The Doings of a Night

It was soon found that the camping ground possessed another advantage which, during the discussion, had been altogether overlooked.

During the afternoon they had shot a fine-looking antelope, cooking a portion at the time upon the prairie. A goodly portion was left, and they now had an opportunity of kindling their fire without the liability of its being seen, as would have been the case had they encamped in any other place.

This being agreed to, the fire was speedily kindled, and the trapper himself began the culinary performance. It was executed with the characteristic excellence of the hunter, and a luscious meal was thus provided for all. At its conclusion, all stretched themselves upon the ground for the purpose of smoking and chatting, as was their usual custom at such times.

The evening whiled pleasantly away, and when it had considerably advanced, the question of who should act as sentinel was discussed. Up to this, young Brainerd had never once performed that duty at night, although he had frequently solicited the privilege. He now asked permission to try his hand. After considerable talk it was agreed that he might do. The trapper had lost so much sleep, that he was anxious to secure a good night's rest, and the careful scrutiny which he had taken of the surrounding prairie convinced him that no danger threatened. So he felt little apprehension in acceding to the wish of the boy.

At a late hour the two men stretched themselves upon the ground, with their blankets gathered about them, and they were soon wrapped in profound slumber, while Johnny, filled with the importance and responsibility of his duty, felt as though he should never need another hour's sleep. He was sure of being able to keep up an unintermitting watch several days and nights, should it become necessary.

Following the usual custom of sentinels, he shouldered his gun and paced back and forth before the smoldering camp-fire, glancing in every direction, so as to make sure that no enemy stole upon him unawares.

It formed a curious picture, the small fire burning in the valley, motionless forms stretched out before it, the huge steam man silent and grim standing near, the dwarfed boy, pacing slowly back and forth, and, above all, the moon shining down upon the silent prairie. The moon was quite faint, so that only an indistinct view of objects could be seen. Occasionally Johnny clambered up the bank and took a survey of the surrounding plains; but seeing nothing at all suspicious, he soon grew weary of this, and confined his walks to the immediate vicinity of the camp-fire, passing back and forth between the narrow breadth of the valley.

As the hours dragged slowly by, the boy gradually fell into a reverie, which made him almost unconscious of external things. And it was while walking thus that he did not observe a large wolf advance to the edge of the gully, look down, and then whisk back out of sight before the sentinel wheeled in his walk and faced him.

Three separate times was this repeated, the wolf looking down in such an earnest, searching way that it certainly would have excited the remark and curiosity of any one observing it. The third glance apparently satisfied the wolf; for it lasted for a few seconds, when he withdrew, and lumbered away at an awkward rate, until a rod or two had been passed, when the supposed wolf suddenly rose on its hind legs, the skin and head were shifted to the arms of the Indian, and he continued on at a leisurely gait until he joined fully fifty comrades, who were huddled together in a grove, several hundred yards away.

In the meantime young Brainerd, with his rifle slung over his shoulder, was pacing back and forth in the same deliberate manner, his mind busily engaged on an "improvement" upon the steam man, by which he was to walk backward as well as forward, although he couldn't satisfactorily determine how he was to go up and down hill with safety.

Still occupied in the study of the subject, he took a seat by the half-extinguished camp-fire and gazed dreamily into the embers. It had been a habit with him, when at home, to sit thus for hours, on the long winter evenings, while his mind was so busily at work that he was totally oblivious to whatever was passing around him.

It must have been that the boy seated himself without any thought of the inevitable result of doing so; for none knew better than he that such a thing was fatal to the faithful performance of a sentinel's duty: and the thought that his three companions, in one sense, had put their safety in his hands, would have prevented anything like a forgetfulness of duty.

Be that as it may, the boy had sat thus less than half an hour when a drowsiness began stealing over him. Once he raised his head and fancied he saw a large wolf glaring down upon him from the bank above, but the head was withdrawn so quickly that he was sure it was only a phantom of his brain.

So he did not rise from his seat, but sitting still he gradually sunk lower, until in a short time he was sleeping as soundly as either of the three around him.

Another hour wore away, and the fire smoldered lower and all was still.

Then numerous heads peered over the edge of the ravine for a few seconds, and as suddenly withdrew.

A few minutes later a curious sight might have been seen, a sight somewhat resembling that of a parcel of school-boys making their gigantic snow-balls. The fifty Indians, the greater portion of whom had patiently waited in the adjoining grove, while their horses were securely fastened near, issued like a swarm of locusts and began rolling huge boulders toward the valley. Some of them were so large that half a dozen only succeeded in moving them with the greatest difficulty.

But they persevered, working with a strange persistency and silence, that gave them the appearance of so many phantoms engaged at their ghostly labor. Not a word was exchanged, even in the most guarded of tones, for each understood his part.

In time half a dozen of these immense stones reached the edge of the ravine. They were ranged side by side, a few feet apart, so as not to be in each other's way, and the Indians stood near, waiting until their work should be completed.

Some signal was then made, and then one of these boulders rolled down in the ravine. Even this scarcely made any percep-tible noise, the yielding ground receiving it like a cushion, as it came to a halt near the center of the valley.

When this was done a second followed suit, being so guided that it did not grate against its companion, but came to rest very near it.

Then another followed, and then another and another, in the same stealthy manner, until over a dozen were in the valley below.

This completed, the phantom-like figures descended like so many shadows, and began tugging again at the boulders.

Not a word was exchanged, for each knew what was required of him. Fully an hour more was occupied, by which time the labor was finished.

The boulders were arranged in the form of an impassable wall across the narrow valley, and the steam man was so thoroughly imprisoned that no human aid could ever extricate him.

# CHAPTER XX

## The Concluding Catastrophe

Baldy Bicknell, the trapper, was the first to discover the peril of himself and party.

When the Indians had completed their work it lacked only an hour of daylight. Having done all that was necessary, the savages took their stations behind the wall, lying flat upon the ground, where they were invisible to the whites, but where every motion of theirs could be watched and checkmated.

When the trapper opened his eyes he did not stir a limb, a way into which he had got during his long experience on the frontiers. He merely moved his head from side to side, so as to see anything that was to be seen.

The first object that met his eye was the boy Brainerd, sound asleep. Apprehensive then that something had occurred, he turned his startled gaze in different directions, scanning everything as well as it could be done in the pale moonlight.

When he caught sight of the wall stretched across the valley, he rubbed his eyes, and looked at it again and again, scarcely able to credit his senses. He was sure it was not there a few hours before, and he could not comprehend what it could mean; but it was a verity, and his experience told him that it could be the work of no one except the Indians, who had outwitted him at last.

His first feeling was that of indignation toward the boy who had permitted this to take place while he was asleep, but his mind quickly turned upon the more important matter of meeting the peril, which, beyond all doubt, was of the most serious character.

As yet he had not stirred his body, and looking toward the

prison wall, he caught a glimpse of the phantom-like figures, as they occasionally flitted about, securing the best possible position, before the whites should awake.

This glimpse made everything plain to the practical mind of Baldy Bicknell. He comprehended that the red-skins had laid a plan to entrap the steam man. More than to entrap themselves, and that, so far as he could judge, they had succeeded completely.

It was the tightest fix in which he had ever been caught, and his mind, fertile as it was in expedients at such crises, could see no way of meeting the danger.

He knew the Indians had horses somewhere at command, while neither he nor his comrades had a single one. The steam man would be unable to pass that formidable wall, as it was not to be supposed that he had been taught the art of leaping.

Whatever plan of escape was determined upon, it was evident that the steamer would have to be abandoned; and this necessitated, as an inevitable consequence, that the whites would have to depend upon their legs. The Missouri river was at no great distance, and if left undisturbed they could make it without difficulty, but there was a prospect of anything sooner than that they would be allowed to depart in peace, after leaving the steam man behind.

The trapper, as had been his invariable custom, had carefully noted the contour of the surrounding prairie, before they had committed the important act of encamping in the gorge or hollow. He remembered the grove at some distance, and was satisfied that the barbarians had left their horses there, while they had gathered behind the wall to wait the critical moment.

By the time these thoughts had fairly taken shape in his brain it was beginning to grow light, and with a premonitary yawn and kick he rose to his feet and began stirring the fire. He was well aware that although he and his companions were a fair target for the rifles of their enemies, yet they would not fire. Their plan of action did not comprehend that, though it would have settled everything in their favor without delay.

"I declare I have been asleep!" exclaimed Brainerd, as he began rubbing his eyes.

"Yes. You're a purty feller to make a sentinel of, ain't you?" replied the trapper, in disgust.

"I hope nothing has happened," answered Johnny, feeling that he deserved all the blame that could be laid upon him.

"Not much, exceptin' while yer war snoozin' the reds have come down and got us all in a nice box."

The boy was certain he was jesting until he saw the expression of his face.

"Surely, Baldy, it is not as bad as that?"

"Do you see that ar'?" demanded the trapper, pointing toward the wall, which the youngster could not help observing.

"How comes that to be there?"

"The red-skins put it thar. Can yer steam man walk over that?"

"Certainly not; but we can remove them."

"Do yer want to try it, younker?"

"I'm willing to help."

"Do yer know that ar' somethin' less nor a hundred redskins ahind them, jist waitin' fur yer to try that thing?"

"Good heavens! can it be possible?"

"Ef you don't b'l'eve it, go out and look for yerself, that's all."

The boy, for the first time, comprehends the peril in which he had brought his friends by his own remissness, and his self-accusation was so great, that, for a few moments, he forgot the fact that he was exposed to the greatest danger of his life.

By this time Ethan and Mickey awoke, and were soon made to understand their predicament. As a matter of course, they were all disposed to blame the author of this; but when they saw how deeply he felt his own shortcoming, all three felt a natural sympathy for him.

"There's no use of talkin' how we came to get hyar," was the philosophical remark of the trapper; "it's 'nough to know that we are hyar, with a mighty slim chance of ever gettin' out ag'in."

"It's enough to make a chap feel down in the mouth, as me friend Jonah observed when he went down the throat of the whale," said Mickey.

"How is it they don't shoot us?" asked Hopkins; "we can't git out of their way, and they've got us in fair range."

"What's the use of doin' that? Ef they kill us, that'll be the end on't; but ef they put thar claws on us, they've got us sure, and can have a good time toastin' us while they yelp and dance around."

All shuddered at the fearful picture drawn by the hunter.

"Jerusalem! don't I wish I was to hum in Connecticut!"

"And it's myself that would be plaised to be sitting in the parlor at Ballyduff wid me own Bridget Moghlaghigbogh, listenin' while she breathed swate vows, after making her supper upon praties and inions."

"I think I'd ruther be hyar," was the commentary of the trapper upon the expressed wish of the Irishman.

"Why can't yees touch up the staamman, and make him hop owver them shtones?" asked Mickey, turning toward the boy, whom, it was noted, appeared to be in deep reverie again.

Not until he was addressed several times did he look up. Then he merely shook his head, to signify that the thing was impossible.

"Any fool might know better than that," remarked the Yankee, "for if he could jump over, where would be the wagon?"

"That 'ud foller, av coorse."

"No; there's no way of getting the steam man out of here. He is a gone case, sure, and it looks as though we were ditto. Jerusalem! I wish all the gold was back in Wolf Ravine, and we war a thousand miles from this place."

"Wishing'll do no good; there's only one chance I see, and that ain't no chance at all."

All, including the boy, eagerly looked up to hear the explanation.

"Some distance from hyar is some timbers, and in thar the reds have left their animals. Ef we start on a run for the timbers, git thar ahead of the Ingins, mount thar hosses and put, thar'll be some chance. Yer can see what chance thar is fur that."

It looked as hopeless as the charge of the Light Brigade.

Young Brainerd now spoke.

"It was I who got you into trouble, and it is I, that, with the blessing of Heaven, am going to get you out of it."

The three now looked eagerly at him.

"Is there no danger of the Indians firing upon us?" he asked of the hunter.

"Not unless we try to run away."

"All right; it is time to begin."

The boy's first proceeding was to kindle a fire in the boiler of the steam man. When it was fairly blazing, he continued to heap in wood, until a fervent heat was produced such as it had never experienced before. Still he threw in wood, and kept the water low in the boiler, until there was a most prodigious pressure of steam, making its escape at half a dozen orifices.

When all the wood was thrown in that it could contain, and portions of the iron sheeting could be seen becoming red-hot, he ceased this, and began trying the steam.

"How much can he hold?" inquired Hopkins.

"One hundred and fifty pounds."

"How much is on now?"

"One hundred and forty-eight, and rising."

"Good heavens! it will blow up!" was the exclamation, as the three shrunk back, appalled at the danger.

"Not for a few minutes; have you the gold secured, and the guns, so as to be ready to run?"

They were ready to run at any moment; the gold was always secured about their persons and it required but a moment to snatch up the weapons.

"When it blows up, run!" was the admonition of the boy.

The steam man was turned directly toward the wall, and a full head of steam let on. It started away with a bound, instantly reaching a speed of forty miles an hour.

The next moment it struck the boulders with a terrific crash, shot on over its face, leaving the splintered wagon behind, and at the instant of touching ground upon the opposite side directly among the thunderstruck Indians, it exploded its boiler!

The shock of the explosion was terrible. It was like the bursting of an immense bomb-shell, the steam man being blown into thousands of fragments, that scattered death and destruction in every direction. Falling in the very center of the crouching Indians, it could but make a terrible destruction of life, while those who escaped unharmed, were beside themselves with consternation.

This was the very thing upon which young Brainerd had counted, and for which he made his calculations. When he saw it leap toward the wall in such a furious manner, he knew the inevitable consequence, and gave the word to his friends to take to their legs.

All three dashed up the bank, and reaching the surface of the prairie, Baldy Bicknell took the lead, exclaiming:

"Now fur the wood yonder!"

As they reached the grove, one or two of the number glanced back, but saw nothing of the pursuing Indians. They had not yet recovered from their terror.

Not a moment was to be lost. The experienced eye of the trapper lost no time in selecting the very best Indian horses, and a moment later all four rode out from the grove at a full gallop, and headed toward the Missouri.

The precise result of the steam man's explosion was never learned. How many were killed and wounded could only be conjectured; but the number certainly was so great that our friends saw nothing more of them.

They evidently had among their number those who had become pretty well acquainted with the steam man, else they would not have laid the plan which they did for capturing him.

Being well mounted, the party made the entire journey to Independence on horseback. From this point they took passage to St. Louis, where the gold was divided, and the party separated, and since then have seen nothing of each other.

Mickey McSquizzle returned to Ballyduff Kings County, Ireland, where, we heard, he and his gentle Bridget, are in the full enjoyment of the three thousand pounds he carried with him.

Ethan Hopkins settled down with the girl of his choice in Connecticut, where, at last accounts, he was doing as well as could be expected.

Baldy Bicknell, although quite a wealthy man, still clings to his wandering habits, and spends the greater portion of his time on the prairies.

With the large amount of money realized from his western trip, Johnny Brainerd is educating himself at one of the best schools in the country. When he shall have completed his course, it is his intention to construct another steam man, capable of more wonderful performances than the first.

So let our readers and the public generally be on the lookout.

## THE END

A CATALOG OF SELECTED

# DOVER BOOKS

IN ALL FIELDS OF INTEREST

# A CATALOG OF SELECTED DOVER
# BOOKS IN ALL FIELDS OF INTEREST

100 BEST-LOVED POEMS, Edited by Philip Smith. "The Passionate Shepherd to His Love," "Shall I compare thee to a summer's day?" "Death, be not proud," "The Raven," "The Road Not Taken," plus works by Blake, Wordsworth, Byron, Shelley, Keats, many others. Includes 13 selections from the Common Core State Standards Initiative. 112pp. 0-486-28553-7

ABC BOOK OF EARLY AMERICANA, Eric Sloane. Artist and historian Eric Sloane presents a wondrous A-to-Z collection of American innovations, including hex signs, ear trumpets, popcorn, and rocking chairs. Illustrated, hand-lettered pages feature brief captions explaining objects' origins and uses. 64pp. 0-486-49808-5

ADVENTURES OF HUCKLEBERRY FINN, Mark Twain. Join Huck and Jim as their boyhood adventures along the Mississippi River lead them into a world of excitement, danger, and self-discovery. Humorous narrative, lyrical descriptions of the Mississippi valley, and memorable characters. 224pp. 0-486-28061-6

ALICE STARMORE'S BOOK OF FAIR ISLE KNITTING, Alice Starmore. A noted designer from the region of Scotland's Fair Isle explores the history and techniques of this distinctive, stranded-color knitting style and provides copious illustrated instructions for 14 original knitwear designs. 208pp. 0-486-47218-3

ALICE'S ADVENTURES IN WONDERLAND, Lewis Carroll. Beloved classic about a little girl lost in a topsy-turvy land and her encounters with the White Rabbit, March Hare, Mad Hatter, Cheshire Cat, and other delightfully improbable characters. 42 illustrations by Sir John Tenniel. A selection of the Common Core State Standards Initiative. 96pp. 0-486-27543-4

THE ARTHUR RACKHAM TREASURY: 86 Full-Color Illustrations, Arthur Rackham. Selected and Edited by Jeff A. Menges. A stunning treasury of 86 full-page plates span the famed English artist's career, from *Rip Van Winkle* (1905) to masterworks such as *Undine*, *A Midsummer Night's Dream*, and *Wind in the Willows* (1939). 96pp. 0-486-44685-9

THE AWAKENING, Kate Chopin. First published in 1899, this controversial novel of a New Orleans wife's search for love outside a stifling marriage shocked readers. Today, it remains a first-rate narrative with superb characterization. New introductory note. 128pp. 0-486-27786-0

BASEBALL IS . . .: Defining the National Pastime, Edited by Paul Dickson. Wisecracking, philosophical, nostalgic, and entertaining, these hundreds of quips and observations by players, their wives, managers, authors, and others cover every aspect of our national pastime. It's a great any-occasion gift for fans! 256pp. 0-486-48209-X

THE CALL OF THE WILD, Jack London. A classic novel of adventure, drawn from London's own experiences as a Klondike adventurer, relating the story of a heroic dog caught in the brutal life of the Alaska Gold Rush. Note. 64pp. 0-486-26472-6

CANDIDE, Voltaire. Edited by Francois-Marie Arouet. One of the world's great satires since its first publication in 1759. Witty, caustic skewering of romance, science, philosophy, religion, government — nearly all human ideals and institutions. A selection of the Common Core State Standards Initiative. 112pp. 0-486-26689-3

THE CARTOON HISTORY OF TIME, Kate Charlesworth and John Gribbin. Cartoon characters explain cosmology, quantum physics, and other concepts covered by Stephen Hawking's *A Brief History of Time*. Humorous graphic novel–style treatment, perfect for young readers and curious folk of all ages. 64pp. 0-486-49097-1

THE CHERRY ORCHARD, Anton Chekhov. Classic of world drama concerns passing of semifeudal order in turn-of-the-century Russia, symbolized in the sale of the cherry orchard owned by Madame Ranevskaya. Showcases Chekhov's rich sensitivities as an observer of human nature. 64pp. 0-486-26682-6

A CHRISTMAS CAROL, Charles Dickens. This engrossing tale relates Ebenezer Scrooge's ghostly journeys through Christmases past, present, and future and his ultimate transformation from a harsh and grasping old miser to a charitable and compassionate human being. 80pp. 0-486-26865-9

CRIME AND PUNISHMENT, Fyodor Dostoyevsky. Translated by Constance Garnett. Supreme masterpiece tells the story of Raskolnikov, a student tormented by his own thoughts after he murders an old woman. Overwhelmed by guilt and terror, he confesses and goes to prison. A selection of the Common Core State Standards Initiative. 448pp. 0-486-41587-2

CYRANO DE BERGERAC, Edmond Rostand. A quarrelsome, hot-tempered, and unattractive swordsman falls hopelessly in love with a beautiful woman and woos her for a handsome but slow-witted suitor. A witty and eloquent drama. 144pp. 0-486-41119-2

A DOLL'S HOUSE, Henrik Ibsen. Ibsen's best-known play displays his genius for realistic prose drama. An expression of women's rights, the play climaxes when the central character, Nora, rejects a smothering marriage and life in "a doll's house." A selection of the Common Core State Standards Initiative. 80pp. 0-486-27062-9

DOOMED SHIPS: Great Ocean Liner Disasters, William H. Miller, Jr. Nearly 200 photographs, many from private collections, highlight tales of some of the vessels whose pleasure cruises ended in catastrophe: the *Morro Castle*, *Normandie*, *Andrea Doria*, *Europa*, and many others. 128pp. 0-486-45366-9

DUBLINERS, James Joyce. A fine and accessible introduction to the work of one of the 20th century's most influential writers, this collection features 15 tales, including a masterpiece of the short-story genre, "The Dead." 160pp. 0-486-26870-5

THE EARLY SCIENCE FICTION OF PHILIP K. DICK, Philip K. Dick. This anthology presents short stories and novellas that originally appeared in pulp magazines of the early 1950s, including "The Variable Man," "Second Variety," "Beyond the Door," "The Defenders," and more. 272pp. 0-486-49733-X

THE EARLY SHORT STORIES OF F. SCOTT FITZGERALD, F. Scott Fitzgerald. These tales offer insights into many themes, characters, and techniques that emerged in Fitzgerald's later works. Selections include "The Curious Case of Benjamin Button," "Babes in the Woods," and a dozen others. 256pp. 0-486-79465-2

ETHAN FROME, Edith Wharton. Classic story of wasted lives, set against a bleak New England background. Superbly delineated characters in a hauntingly grim tale of thwarted love. Considered by many to be Wharton's masterpiece. 96pp. 0-486-26690-7

FLATLAND: A Romance of Many Dimensions, Edwin A. Abbott. Classic of science (and mathematical) fiction — charmingly illustrated by the author — describes the adventures of A. Square, a resident of Flatland, in Spaceland (three dimensions), Lineland (one dimension), and Pointland (no dimensions). 96pp. 0-486-27263-X

FRANKENSTEIN, Mary Shelley. The story of Victor Frankenstein's monstrous creation and the havoc it caused has enthralled generations of readers and inspired countless writers of horror and suspense. With the author's own 1831 introduction. 176pp. 0-486-28211-2

THE GARGOYLE BOOK: 572 Examples from Gothic Architecture, Lester Burbank Bridaham. Dispelling the conventional wisdom that French Gothic architectural flourishes were born of despair or gloom, Bridaham reveals the whimsical nature of these creations and the ingenious artisans who made them. 572 illustrations. 224pp. 0-486-44754-5

THE GIFT OF THE MAGI AND OTHER SHORT STORIES, O. Henry. Sixteen captivating stories by one of America's most popular storytellers. Included are such classics
as "The Gift of the Magi," "The Last Leaf," and "The Ransom of Red Chief." Publisher's
Note. A selection of the Common Core State Standards Initiative. 96pp. 0-486-27061-0

THE GOETHE TREASURY: Selected Prose and Poetry, Johann Wolfgang von Goethe.
Edited, Selected, and with an Introduction by Thomas Mann. In addition to his lyric
poetry, Goethe wrote travel sketches, autobiographical studies, essays, letters, and
proverbs in rhyme and prose. This collection presents outstanding examples from
each genre. 368pp. 0-486-44780-4

GREAT ILLUSTRATIONS BY N. C. WYETH, N. C. Wyeth. Edited and with an
Introduction by Jeff A. Menges. This full-color collection focuses on the artist's early
and most popular illustrations, featuring more than 100 images from *The Mysterious
Stranger, Robin Hood, Robinson Crusoe, The Boy's King Arthur*, and other classics. 128pp.
0-486-47295-7

HAMLET, William Shakespeare. The quintessential Shakespearean tragedy, whose
highly charged confrontations and anguished soliloquies probe depths of human feeling rarely sounded in any art. Reprinted from an authoritative British edition complete with illuminating footnotes. A selection of the Common Core State Standards
Initiative. 128pp. 0-486-27278-8

THE HAUNTED HOUSE, Charles Dickens. A Yuletide gathering in an eerie country retreat provides the backdrop for Dickens and his friends — including Elizabeth
Gaskell and Wilkie Collins — who take turns spinning supernatural yarns. 144pp.
0-486-46309-5

HEART OF DARKNESS, Joseph Conrad. Dark allegory of a journey up the Congo
River and the narrator's encounter with the mysterious Mr. Kurtz. Masterly blend of
adventure, character study, psychological penetration. For many, Conrad's finest, most
enigmatic story. 80pp. 0-486-26464-5

THE HOUND OF THE BASKERVILLES, Sir Arthur Conan Doyle. A deadly curse
in the form of a legendary ferocious beast continues to claim its victims from the
Baskerville family until Holmes and Watson intervene. Often called the best detective
story ever written. 128pp. 0-486-28214-7

THE HOUSE BEHIND THE CEDARS, Charles W. Chesnutt. Originally published in
1900, this groundbreaking novel by a distinguished African-American author recounts
the drama of a brother and sister who "pass for white" during the dangerous days of
Reconstruction. 208pp. 0-486-46144-0

HOW TO DRAW NEARLY EVERYTHING, Victor Perard. Beginners of all ages can
learn to draw figures, faces, landscapes, trees, flowers, and animals of all kinds. Well-
illustrated guide offers suggestions for pencil, pen, and brush techniques plus compo-
sition, shading, and perspective. 160pp. 0-486-49848-4

HOW TO MAKE SUPER POP-UPS, Joan Irvine. Illustrated by Linda Hendry. Super
pop-ups extend the element of surprise with three-dimensional designs that slide,
turn, spring, and snap. More than 30 patterns and 475 illustrations include cards,
stage props, and school projects. 96pp. 0-486-46589-6

THE IMITATION OF CHRIST, Thomas à Kempis. Translated by Aloysius Croft and
Harold Bolton. This religious classic has brought understanding and comfort to mil-
lions for centuries. Written in a candid and conversational style, the topics include
liberation from worldly inclinations, preparation and consolations of prayer, and eu-
charistic communion. 160pp. 0-486-43185-1

Browse over 10,000 books at www.doverpublications.com

CATALOG OF DOVER BOOKS

THE IMPORTANCE OF BEING EARNEST, Oscar Wilde. Wilde's witty and buoyant comedy of manners, filled with some of literature's most famous epigrams, reprinted from an authoritative British edition. Considered Wilde's most perfect work. A selection of the Common Core State Standards Initiative. 64pp. 0-486-26478-5

JANE EYRE, Charlotte Brontë. Written in 1847, *Jane Eyre* tells the tale of an orphan girl's progress from the custody of cruel relatives to an oppressive boarding school and its culmination in a troubled career as a governess. A selection of the Common Core State Standards Initiative. 448pp. 0-486-42449-9

JUST WHAT THE DOCTOR DISORDERED: Early Writings and Cartoons of Dr. Seuss, Dr. Seuss. Edited and with an Introduction by Rick Marschall. The Doctor's visual hilarity, nonsense language, and offbeat sense of humor illuminate this compilation of items from his early career, created for periodicals such as *Judge, Life, College Humor,* and *Liberty.* 144pp. 0-486-49846-8

KING LEAR, William Shakespeare. Powerful tragedy of an aging king, betrayed by his daughters, robbed of his kingdom, descending into madness. Perhaps the bleakest of Shakespeare's tragic dramas, complete with explanatory footnotes. 144pp. 0-486-28058-6

THE LADY OR THE TIGER?: and Other Logic Puzzles, Raymond M. Smullyan. Created by a renowned puzzle master, these whimsically themed challenges involve paradoxes about probability, time, and change; metapuzzles; and self-referentiality. Nineteen chapters advance in difficulty from relatively simple to highly complex. 1982 edition. 240pp.
0-486-47027-X

LEAVES OF GRASS: The Original 1855 Edition, Walt Whitman. Whitman's immortal collection includes some of the greatest poems of modern times, including his masterpiece, "Song of Myself." Shattering standard conventions, it stands as an unabashed celebration of body and nature. 128pp. 0-486-45676-5

LES MISÉRABLES, Victor Hugo. Translated by Charles E. Wilbour. Abridged by James K. Robinson. A convict's heroic struggle for justice and redemption plays out against a fiery backdrop of the Napoleonic wars. This edition features the excellent original translation and a sensitive abridgment. 304pp. 0-486-45789-3

LIGHT FOR THE ARTIST, Ted Seth Jacobs. Intermediate and advanced art students receive a broad vocabulary of effects with this in-depth study of light. Diagrams and paintings illustrate applications of principles to figure, still life, and landscape paintings. 144pp. 0-486-49304-0

LILITH: A Romance, George MacDonald. In this novel by the father of fantasy literature, a man travels through time to meet Adam and Eve and to explore humanity's fall from grace and ultimate redemption. 240pp. 0-486-46818-6

LINE: An Art Study, Edmund J. Sullivan. Written by a noted artist and teacher, this well-illustrated guide introduces the basics of line drawing. Topics include third and fourth dimensions, formal perspective, shade and shadow, figure drawing, and other essentials. 208pp. 0-486-79484-9

THE LODGER, Marie Belloc Lowndes. Acclaimed by *The New York Times* as "one of the best suspense novels ever written," this novel recounts an English couple's doubts about their boarder, whom they suspect of being a serial killer. 240pp. 0-486-78809-1

MACBETH, William Shakespeare. A Scottish nobleman murders the king in order to succeed to the throne. Tortured by his conscience and fearful of discovery, he becomes tangled in a web of treachery and deceit that ultimately spells his doom. A selection of the Common Core State Standards Initiative. 96pp. 0-486-27802-6

MANHATTAN IN MAPS 1527–2014, Paul E. Cohen and Robert T. Augustyn. This handsome volume features 65 full-color maps charting Manhattan's development from the first Dutch settlement to the present. Each map is placed in context by an accompanying essay. 176pp. 0-486-77991-2

MEDEA, Euripides. One of the most powerful and enduring of Greek tragedies, masterfully portraying the fierce motives driving Medea's pursuit of vengeance for her husband's insult and betrayal. Authoritative Rex Warner translation. 64pp. 0-486-27548-5

THE METAMORPHOSIS AND OTHER STORIES, Franz Kafka. Excellent new English translations of title story (considered by many critics Kafka's most perfect work), plus "The Judgment," "In the Penal Colony," "A Country Doctor," and "A Report to an Academy." A selection of the Common Core State Standards Initiative. 96pp. 0-486-29030-1

METROPOLIS, Thea von Harbou. This Weimar-era novel of a futuristic society, written by the screenwriter for the iconic 1927 film, was hailed by noted science-fiction authority Forrest J. Ackerman as "a work of genius." 224pp. 0-486-79567-5

THE MYSTERIOUS MICKEY FINN, Elliot Paul. A multimillionaire's disappearance incites a maelstrom of kidnapping, murder, and a plot to restore the French monarchy. "One of the funniest books we've read in a long time." — *The New York Times.* 256pp. 0-486-24751-1

NARRATIVE OF THE LIFE OF FREDERICK DOUGLASS, Frederick Douglass. The impassioned abolitionist and eloquent orator provides graphic descriptions of his childhood and horrifying experiences as a slave as well as a harrowing record of his dramatic escape to the North and eventual freedom. A selection of the Common Core State Standards Initiative. 96pp. 0-486-28499-9

OBELISTS FLY HIGH, C. Daly King. Masterpiece of detective fiction portrays murder aboard a 1935 transcontinental flight. Combining an intricate plot and "locked room" scenario, the mystery was praised by *The New York Times* as "a very thrilling story." 288pp. 0-486-25036-9

THE ODYSSEY, Homer. Excellent prose translation of ancient epic recounts adventures of the homeward-bound Odysseus. Fantastic cast of gods, giants, cannibals, sirens, other supernatural creatures — true classic of Western literature. A selection of the Common Core State Standards Initiative. 256pp. 0-486-40654-7

OEDIPUS REX, Sophocles. Landmark of Western drama concerns the catastrophe that ensues when King Oedipus discovers he has inadvertently killed his father and married his mother. Masterly construction, dramatic irony. A selection of the Common Core State Standards Initiative. 64pp. 0-486-26877-2

OTHELLO, William Shakespeare. Towering tragedy tells the story of a Moorish general who earns the enmity of his ensign Iago when he passes him over for a promotion. Masterly portrait of an archvillain. Explanatory footnotes. 112pp. 0-486-29097-2

THE PICTURE OF DORIAN GRAY, Oscar Wilde. Celebrated novel involves a handsome young Londoner who sinks into a life of depravity. His body retains perfect youth and vigor while his recent portrait reflects the ravages of his crime and sensuality. 176pp. 0-486-27807-7

A PLACE CALLED PECULIAR: Stories About Unusual American Place-Names, Frank K. Gallant. From Smut Eye, Alabama, to Tie Siding, Wyoming, this pop-culture history offers a well-written and highly entertaining survey of America's most unusual place-names and their often-humorous origins. 256pp. 0-486-48360-6

PRIDE AND PREJUDICE, Jane Austen. One of the most universally loved and admired English novels, an effervescent tale of rural romance transformed by Jane Austen's art into a witty, shrewdly observed satire of English country life. A selection of the Common Core State Standards Initiative. 272pp. 0-486-28473-5

**Browse over 10,000 books at www.doverpublications.com**

SIDDHARTHA, Hermann Hesse. Classic novel that has inspired generations of seekers. Blending Eastern mysticism and psychoanalysis, Hesse presents a strikingly original view of man and culture and the arduous process of self-discovery, reconciliation, harmony, and peace. 112pp. 0-486-40653-9

SKETCHING OUTDOORS, Leonard Richmond. This guide offers beginners step-by-step demonstrations of how to depict clouds, trees, buildings, and other outdoor sights. Explanations of a variety of techniques include shading and constructional drawing. 48pp. 0-486-46922-0

SKETCHING THE COUNTRYSIDE: How to Draw the Vanishing Rural Landscape, Frank J. Lohan. Both experienced and aspiring artists can benefit from this practical guide. More than 400 detailed illustrations include fundamentals for drawing trees, rocks, buildings, mountains, lakes, and other scenic elements. 272pp. 0-486-47887-4

SMALL HOUSES OF THE FORTIES: With Illustrations and Floor Plans, Harold E. Group. 56 floor plans and elevations of houses that originally cost less than $15,000 to build. Recommended by financial institutions of the era, they range from Colonials to Cape Cods. 144pp. 0-486-45598-X

SONGS FOR THE OPEN ROAD: Poems of Travel and Adventure, Edited by The American Poetry & Literacy Project. More than 80 poems by 50 American and British masters celebrate real and metaphorical journeys. Poems by Whitman, Byron, Millay, Sandburg, Langston Hughes, Emily Dickinson, Robert Frost, Shelley, Tennyson, Yeats, many others. Includes 4 selections from the Common Core State Standards Initiative. 80pp. 0-486-40646-6

SPEAKING FOR NATURE: The Literary Naturalists, from Transcendentalism to the Birth of the American Environmental Movement, Paul Brooks. With a new Foreword by Linda Lear. Narrative portraits of America's great literary naturalists offer a 200-year history of wildlife conservation: Thoreau, Burroughs, Muir, Beebe, Carson, and many others. "Brisk and illuminating." — *The New York Times Book Review*. 320pp. 0-486-78143-7

SPOON RIVER ANTHOLOGY, Edgar Lee Masters. An American poetry classic, in which former citizens of a mythical midwestern town speak touchingly from the grave of the thwarted hopes and dreams of their lives. 144pp. 0-486-27275-3

STAR LORE: Myths, Legends, and Facts, William Tyler Olcott. Captivating retellings of the origins and histories of ancient star groups include Pegasus, Ursa Major, Pleiades, signs of the zodiac, and other constellations. "Classic." — *Sky & Telescope*. 58 illustrations. 544pp. 0-486-43581-4

THE STRANGE CASE OF DR. JEKYLL AND MR. HYDE, Robert Louis Stevenson. This intriguing novel, both fantasy thriller and moral allegory, depicts the struggle of two opposing personalities — one essentially good, the other evil — for the soul of one man. 64pp. 0-486-26688-5

STRIP FOR MURDER, Max Allan Collins. Illustrated by Terry Beatty. Colorful characters with murderous motives populate this illustrated mystery, in which the heated rivalry between a pair of cartoonists ends in homicide and a stripper-turned-detective and her stepson-partner seek the killer. "Great fun." — *Mystery Scene*. 288pp. 0-486-79811-9

THE SUN, THE IDEA & STORY WITHOUT WORDS: Three Graphic Novels, Frans Masereel. With a New Introduction by David A. Beronä. Three wordless novels by a master, told in 206 Expressionistic woodcuts: *The Sun*, a struggle with destiny; *The Idea*, a concept's triumph oversuppression; and *Story Without Words*, a poignant romance. Contains adult material. 224pp. 0-486-47169-1

SURVIVAL HANDBOOK: The Official U.S. Army Guide, Department of the Army. This special edition of the Army field manual is geared toward civilians. An essential companion for campers and all lovers of the outdoors, it constitutes the most authoritative wilderness guide. 288pp. 0-486-46184-X

SWEENEY TODD THE STRING OF PEARLS: The Original Victorian Classic, James Malcolm Rymer or Thomas Peckett Prest. Foreword by Rohan McWilliam. The inspiration for a long-running Broadway musical, this Victorian novel in the penny dreadful tradition recounts the nefarious doings of a murderous barber and baker who recycle their victims into meat pies. 304pp. 0-486-79739-2

A TALE OF TWO CITIES, Charles Dickens. Against the backdrop of the French Revolution, Dickens unfolds his masterpiece of drama, adventure, and romance about a man falsely accused of treason. Excitement and derring-do in the shadow of the guillotine. 304pp. 0-486-40651-2

THIRTY YEARS THAT SHOOK PHYSICS: The Story of Quantum Theory, George Gamow. Lucid, accessible introduction to the influential theory of energy and matter features careful explanations of Dirac's anti-particles, Bohr's model of the atom, and much more. Numerous drawings. 1966 edition. 272pp. 0-486-24895-X

TREASURE ISLAND, Robert Louis Stevenson. Classic adventure story of a perilous sea journey, a mutiny led by the infamous Long John Silver, and a lethal scramble for buried treasure — seen through the eyes of cabin boy Jim Hawkins. 160pp. 0-486-27559-0

THE TRIAL, Franz Kafka. Translated by David Wyllie. From its gripping first sentence onward, this novel exemplifies the term "Kafkaesque." Its darkly humorous narrative recounts a bank clerk's entrapment in a bureaucratic maze, based on an undisclosed charge. 176pp. 0-486-47061-X

THE TURN OF THE SCREW, Henry James. Gripping ghost story by great novelist depicts the sinister transformation of 2 innocent children into flagrant liars and hypocrites. An elegantly told tale of unspoken horror and psychological terror. 96pp. 0-486-26684-2

TWELVE YEARS A SLAVE, Solomon Northup. The basis for the Academy Award®-winning movie! Kidnapped into slavery in 1841, Northup spent 12 years in captivity. This autobiographical memoir represents an exceptionally detailed and accurate description of slave life and plantation society. 7 illustrations. Index. 352pp. 0-486-78962-4

VARNEY THE VAMPYRE: or, The Feast of Blood, Part 1, James Malcolm Rymer or Thomas Peckett Prest. With an Introduction by E. F. Bleiler. A deathless creature with an insatiable appetite for blood, Varney is the antihero of this epic, which predates *Dracula* and establishes many of the conventions associated with vampirism. Volume 1 of 2. 480pp. 0-486-22844-4

VARNEY THE VAMPYRE: or, The Feast of Blood, Part 2, James Malcolm Rymer or Thomas Peckett Prest. In this gripping Gothic drama of the 1840s, the bloodthirsty title character repeatedly dies but is reborn and forced to renew his relentless search for victims. Volume 2 of 2. 448pp. 0-486-22845-2

VICTORIAN MURDERESSES: A True History of Thirteen Respectable French and English Women Accused of Unspeakable Crimes, Mary S. Hartman. Riveting combination of true crime and social history examines a dozen famous cases, offering illuminating details of the accused women's backgrounds, deeds, and trials. "Vividly written, meticulously researched." — *Choice.* 336pp. 0-486-78047-3